MAIN STREET
Dealmaker

BRIGHTON WALSH

COPYRIGHT

CHAPTER 1

Sadie Rollins wasn't sure what it was about Christmastime in Havenbrook, but she couldn't deny that it felt as if there were actual magic floating in the air. Snow may have been rare in their pocket of Mississippi, but that didn't stop the holiday spirit from settling over their quaint little town. From Thanksgiving through New Year's, the homes and businesses were decked out with wreaths and garland and enough twinkling lights to be seen from space.

Just exactly how she liked it.

The festiveness wasn't relegated to just outside, though. Since she was little, she'd always loved decorating, and that had only grown now that she had an entire bed-and-breakfast in which to do so. The Starlight Haven Inn's six trees were trimmed within an inch of their lives, garland was draped around each of the plethora of fireplaces in the old Victorian, and fairy lights hung from the ceiling like the icicles they so rarely saw in Mississippi.

She couldn't deny the happiness she felt every morning when she stepped inside. Though maybe that sentiment had nothing at all to do with the decorations and everything to do with the fact that she was in the business of Happily Ever Afters.

"Yes, I'm sure, Naomi," Sadie said into the phone, nodding even though the harried bride on the other end of the line couldn't see her. "All 120 poinsettias you ordered for the gazebo arrived this mornin'. I counted to make sure." Twice.

Naomi exhaled a relieved sigh. "You're a godsend, Sadie. A *godsend*. Have I told you that?"

Sadie laughed. "Not today."

"I'm serious! I have no idea what I'd do if I didn't have you helpin' me with this. Brad's so sick of my craziness."

"I'm sure that future husband of yours isn't sick of anything. And I'm always happy to be able to make things a little easier for you. You can call any time for whatever you need."

"Well..."

Sadie's lips twitched. "Was there something else you were wonderin' about?"

Naomi blew out a sharp breath. "Would you think I was a total diva if I had you go over the schedule one more time?"

"Not at all," Sadie said without hesitation, already pulling up the schedule she'd painstakingly created, down to the minute. "This is your big day, and we want to make sure everything runs smoothly for you."

Timing was a challenge even under the best circumstances, but after planning almost fifty weddings, Sadie knew most didn't come close to the best circumstances. Which was why she had the day detailed within an inch of its life. And also why she had Plans B through Z just in case A didn't go off without a hitch.

She, once again, went over the schedule with Naomi, assuring her everything would be perfect for her special day before ending the call with a promise to check in again tomorrow. Sadie was so comfortable with the task now—both planning the day and dealing with the frantic brides leading up to it—that no one would ever guess she'd fallen into the job when she, along with her twin sister, Elise, had inherited the bed-and-breakfast at the ripe old age of twenty-five.

Three years ago, she'd still been fumbling through her life, trying to figure out what she wanted to do when she grew up. Yes, she had a business degree that had gotten her a job as an office administrator in town, but that hadn't ignited any sort of passion within her. It had been a job, plain and simple. It hadn't been until she'd planned her first wedding at the B&B—full of one mistake after another, but amazing nonetheless—that she could say she'd truly found her calling.

Of course, with as tiny as Havenbrook was, there was no way wedding planning alone—even when one included all events within that distinction—would keep her busy, but the inn itself was enough of a job to fill her days.

Elise rushed out from the tiny back office as she shrugged into her winter coat. "Okay, I'm outta here."

Sadie's brow furrowed as she glanced around the bustling inn. "Where're you goin'?"

The inn was booked solid, as it usually was this time of year. The holidays were one of their highest-grossing seasons, thankfully allowing them to float by in the leaner months. But busy meant Sadie couldn't do this on her own —although her sister definitely pushed those boundaries as much as possible. It wasn't a secret that Elise didn't love the inn like Sadie did. Sometimes she thought her sister would sell the B&B at the first opportunity.

Sadie would find a way to make it work on her own before she ever let that happen.

"I have that thing, remember?" Elise wound a scarf around her neck and fluffed her dyed black hair—so very different from their natural red. A tiny rebellious streak that had started shortly after her divorce.

If Mr. and Mrs. St. Charles weren't sitting in the parlor, drinking their afternoon tea in front of the roaring fire only fifteen feet from where she and her sister stood, Sadie might have snapped back. Instead, she pressed her lips together and forced a smile. "No, I don't. What *thing*?"

"I told you yesterday."

She absolutely did not. "Tell me again."

Elise rolled her eyes. "I promised I'd help Will get things set up for the tree lighting and parade this weekend.

You know how frazzled she always gets during the holidays."

That was certainly true. The festivities in Havenbrook between Thanksgiving and New Year's were even more involved than their Fourth of July celebration, and Willow Haven—their cousin and event coordinator for the town—spent months coordinating that. That wasn't a surprise, considering the Fourth of July lasted a single day and Havenbrook went all out every weekend for more than a month straight during the holidays. Even though she desperately needed Elise's help around the inn, Sadie couldn't fault her for helping their cousin when Will barely stayed afloat this time of year.

She just wished Elise would check once in a while to make sure *she* wasn't the one who was drowning.

Sadie's shoulders slumped as she realized she was on her own. Again. "Yeah. All right. Do you know when you'll be back?" she asked, pulling up the rest of the day's schedule.

"Not really. Why?"

"*Why?*" Sadie gestured to the full, color-coded calendar displayed on the monitor in front of them. "Um, because I'm tryin' to run an inn here, and it'd be great if I could have some help." She pointed to each event on the screen as she recited them, hoping against hope that her sister would wake up from whatever this funk was she'd been in since her divorce and actually...*care* about something. "The day is packed. I need to show Mr. and Mrs. St. Charles to their couple's massage by four, have to confirm the Baumgartners' dinner reservation tonight at six, and then make sure the horse-drawn carriage is here by seven sharp, not to mention we need to start plannin' for the Sip and Shop event in two weeks."

"See? And you've already got this all under control. I'd just get in the way."

"Just because I'm better at the details doesn't give you a free pass to bail," she said, conscious of keeping her voice down so as not to draw attention to them. "While I'm doin' all that, you can handle—" She glanced at the screen, her eyes stuttering over the name blocking out the one and only room they'd converted within the inn to be used as a meeting space.

Okay, so yeah, making her sister help the man who'd represented her ex-husband in their divorce wasn't an option. Although Sadie wasn't exactly a good replacement. Cole Donovan, with all his arrogant, insufferable cockiness, made her blood boil, and that feeling hadn't receded at all in the three years since Elise's divorce.

"See you tomorrow," Elise tossed over her shoulder, fluttering her fingers in a wave as she blew out the front door before Sadie could even sputter a response.

Her mouth dropped open as she watched her brat of a sister flee as if she were running from the scene of a crime. Too bad Sadie couldn't have her arrested for being an asshole.

"You've got to be kiddin' me," she muttered, running her hands through her hair as she surveyed the schedule, which had suddenly morphed from a few hours of her day to another overnight shift.

They'd been bequeathed the inn with nothing but its contents, and the upkeep was astronomical and ate up a good majority of the funds brought in by guests. Without enough cash flow to hire additional staff, she and Elise took turns staying the night in the guest house on the property— or they did in theory, anyway. More often than not, it was Sadie who stayed on-site.

She couldn't say she actually minded too much, though. The cottage was adorable, and she'd considered more than once just biting the bullet and officially moving in. But staying there meant she was on call twenty-four hours a day for whatever issues came up at the inn. True, they were few and far between, but she'd gotten enough 3 a.m. wake-ups that she could say it wasn't exactly peaceful.

"Well, I guess I know what my plans are tonight." She exhaled a sigh, her shoulders slumping as she prepared herself for another long evening.

But it wasn't like she had much else going on. She might have planned forevers for happy couples, but she was nowhere near finding that for herself. In order for that to happen, one needed to actually, you know, date. And Sadie couldn't remember the last time she'd been out on one of those.

Finding her soul mate was definitely on her to-do list, though. You couldn't plan weddings for a living and bear witness to two people promising to share their lives with each other without yearning for the same. She'd just hit a few snags along the way. And by snags, she meant jerks.

Seemed she had a way of attracting them.

No sooner had she thought that than had the master of jerks himself walked out of the inn's makeshift conference room, one of his smarmy clients leading the way.

"You think since I paid for her fake titties, I can get 'em, too? Best thing that ever came out of that prison sentence of a marriage, if you ask me," aforementioned smarmy client said.

"It *would* be a shame for you not to get a souvenir," Cole said, not an ounce of emotion in his voice. "I'll see what I can do."

Ugh. The way they talked about that woman—about that *marriage*—as if both were inconsequential was enough to turn her stomach. It was reason number four thousand and fifty-three why she truly detested Cole Donovan. She couldn't keep the disgust from her face—she always wore her heart on her sleeve, for better or worse—and from the subtle lift of Cole's eyebrow in her direction, every bit of that showed.

She cleared her throat and averted her gaze, focusing her efforts on sorting through the pile of mail Edna had dropped off earlier in the day. As the conversation continued in front of her, she listened with disgust, all the while pretending to be incredibly interested in the latest issue of *Happily Ever After* that had been delivered.

"You think you can get me that, Donovan?"

Sadie's ears perked up. Somewhere along the way,

she'd been pulled into the artfully decorated reception locations and stopped listening to the men's conversation. Were they still talking about his soon-to-be ex-wife's breasts?

Cole paused, then cleared his throat. "If that's what you truly want."

Smarmy guy—Travis—snorted. "I don't give a rat's ass about her doll collection. I just don't want her to have it."

No longer breasts, but something equally infuriating. Sadie ground her molars together so hard her jaw ached. While she hadn't been privy to the specific details surrounding her ex-brother-in-law's sudden obsession with the collection of antique furniture housed in the inn that had been part of their family for generations, she had little doubt the conversation had gone remarkably similarly to the one happening in front of her. Were these men's penises so tiny that they had to overcompensate by stripping their wives of what they loved the most?

She made a disgusted noise in her throat and quickly covered it up with a cough, but not before she'd snagged Cole's attention. He turned his devastating blue eyes on her, and she was so caught off guard, she had to grip the counter just to steady herself.

Why did all the gorgeous men have to be complete pricks?

Cole wore a navy suit, very obviously expensive and very obviously tailored to fit his body like a glove. She averted her gaze before she could catalog the breadth of his shoulders or the planes of his chest beneath the baby-blue button-up he wore. But looking at his face was no better. His dark-blond hair was floppy, almost careless, and a whisper of scruff brushed his chiseled jaw—both of which were incongruent from the otherwise perfection of him. Honestly, was it so much to ask for a freaking scar or something?

Although, she supposed his horrid personality was blemish enough.

"Long as it don't take too long," Travis the Smarmy Jackass was saying. "Wanna be free and clear ASAP. Though that never stopped me before, if you know what I'm sayin'." His lips turned up in a sneer, and he elbowed Cole, intent to bring him in on the joke. "'specially when there're ones as pretty as this just waitin' to get the D." He turned his attention to Sadie and braced his elbows on the front desk, leaning too close for comfort, his wretched breath nearly knocking her over. "What's your name, darlin'? I've got only a few months till this thing is final, but we don't gotta wait that long..."

Sadie bared her teeth in a semblance of a smile, reminding herself that maiming an individual was most definitely a crime. "Such a charming proposition," she said in a voice that dripped faux sweetness, "but I'm gonna have to pass. I don't think my boyfriend would take too kindly to me seein' other men. But I do *so* appreciate the offer."

Travis shrugged, unbothered, no doubt because he'd be dropping those lines again later that evening. For men like that—and no doubt men like Cole Donovan who helped these miserable excuses for human beings—it wasn't about love. It wasn't even about the person. It was about what she could offer him—namely a warm place between her thighs and little else.

Sadie wasn't in the business of one nights. She was in the business of forever. And there was little doubt neither of the two men in front of her could provide that.

CHAPTER 2

I f Cole Donovan had ever doubted that his ex-wife was the actual devil, he had days like this to remind him. There was no other explanation for why he'd been thrust into a situation where he'd be tormented. Tempted, day in and day out, for three solid weeks, with what he absolutely, without a doubt, could not have.

He walked his client, Travis Allen, out of the Starlight Haven Inn, schooling his features as he kept a tight leash on his irritation, despite anger crackling beneath his skin. For years, he'd been able to separate what his clients did and said from what he needed to fight for on their behalf. So then, why was he letting Travis's dick comments get to him?

"What do you think of Red in there?" Travis elbowed Cole in the stomach and nodded back toward the inn. "Think it's natural?"

Clenching his hands into fists, Cole locked his jaw and

reminded himself that his relationship with Travis—both personal and professional—would soon be coming to an end. And then he was *done* doing favors for old friends. He was still feeling the chill courtesy of his last one.

He clapped Travis on the shoulder, much harder than necessary, and barely bit back the smile at the guy's sharp *Oof*. "Just so there's no confusion," he said, his tone low but firm, "I absolutely will not represent you in a sexual harassment case."

Travis chuckled and shook his head. "Aw, c'mon, man. I was just playin' around. She's hot, though, isn't she? A little young and innocent for my usual tastes, but I can definitely work with that. Dirty her up, know what I'm sayin'? Think she was just givin' me a line about havin' a boyfriend?"

Cole refused to look back at Sadie Rollins—aforementioned "young and innocent," his undeclared nemesis, and possibly the most idealistic, not to mention gorgeous, woman he'd ever met. Also, one of a very few people in Havenbrook responsible for keeping him in business.

After all, without marriages, there wouldn't be divorces, and he'd be out of a job.

Sadie might be there to set those couples up with the illusion of their happy ending, but Cole was the one who was around to pick up the pieces when it inevitably fell apart.

"I don't know, and I don't care," Cole said, concealing all emotion in his tone. With a firm hand, he guided Travis toward his ostentatious truck—the one Cole liked to refer to as Travis's Small-Dick Express—eager to put an end to this interaction. "And you shouldn't either. If you want that laundry list of demands from your wife, you better not get caught fucking around in town."

Travis held up his hands. "All right, man. Point taken." He shot finger guns—complete with sound effects—in Cole's direction before opening the door to his jacked-up F-250 and climbing up. "I'm so damn glad we rushed the same fraternity back in the day. I wouldn't be gettin' fuck-all if it weren't for you."

Without another word, Travis slid into the driver's seat before starting the overdone beast and peeling out of the driveway.

"Yeah, that's the problem," Cole muttered to himself as he ran a tired hand through his hair.

Working with people like Travis hadn't always been so exhausting. Ever since his ex-wife—the she-devil—had blindsided him with the one-two punch of sleeping with his former best friend and then serving him with divorce papers after he found out, he'd gladly slid into his role as take-no-prisoners divorce attorney, able to move past that deception by representing men in similar situations and making sure they got their revenge in court. And he'd made a name for himself by doing so. Enough that it was no longer only wronged men who sought him out.

But somehow, revenge wasn't enough anymore. He didn't know what had changed in the past few months, but lately, he'd felt...unsettled. Though, his current upheaval certainly wasn't helping things. Cole didn't do well with change, and he was presently living in a constant state of it, thanks to his temporary home.

He inhaled a few lungfuls of the crisp December air as he pressed his thumb and forefinger to his closed eyes and mentally counted down how many days he had left in this hellhole.

"What're you doin' out here in the cold, sugar?" Edna, Havenbrook's mail carrier, called from her old Jeep before stepping out with a package in tow.

"Afternoon, Edna." He tipped his head at the older woman currently decked out in a flashing holiday sweater that read, *Come deck my halls, Santa*. "How's your day been?"

"It's about to get a lot better." She hooked her hand around Cole's elbow as she not so subtly guided them up the front porch steps and to the inn's entrance. "I always coordinate any package drop-offs with Sadie's afternoon bakin' session. If my calculations are correct—and they are because this isn't my first rodeo—those cookies will still be warm from the oven."

Ah, yes. That which had been tempting him every day since he'd arrived on Monday, the mouthwatering scent making him hungry like he hadn't been in years. Cookies. Yeah, it was definitely the cookies that had evoked that reaction.

"Then we better get you inside." He held open the ornate front door, the carved mahogany no doubt an original fixture of the late-1800's home, as Edna strolled through as if she owned the place. Though, from her outfit that coordinated with the inn's festive interior, he wouldn't be surprised.

Even though it was only a week past Thanksgiving, the front entryway was laden with fresh garland and wreaths, clusters of flickering candles in glass terrariums, and its own tree—one of too damn many to keep track of in the inn. White lights twinkled everywhere his eyes landed as he strode into the main gathering space, the scents of cinnamon and, yep, freshly baked cookies wafting his way.

Okay, so Starlight Haven wasn't actually a hellhole. It was a gorgeous, recently renovated home that had been maintained well. Though, from what he knew of the inn's history, neither that maintenance nor renovation fell at the feet of the woman who was both his biggest irritation and temptation.

"Forgot to drop this off for you earlier, Sadie," Edna said, holding up the package.

"Well, you came at the perfect time. I just took these out of the oven."

"Oh, what luck!"

With a snort, Cole paused just inside the room, his hand in the pocket of his suit pants, and watched Sadie interact with Edna. Her whole face lit up when she spoke to someone she didn't hate—obviously something he didn't usually have the pleasure of witnessing.

Christ, she was gorgeous, all fiery hair, bright blue eyes, and soft pink lips. The worst part about Sadie the Temptress was that she had no idea the power she held. She snagged his attention without even trying—something she'd managed to do nearly every day since he'd moved to Havenbrook shortly after his divorce four years ago.

It was really too bad he'd caught her attention for all the wrong reasons.

They hadn't spoken a single word to each other before they'd officially met when he'd represented her complete asshole of an ex-brother-in-law. But even if they had, it wouldn't have mattered. He could've been a saint—and, to be clear, he absolutely was *not* a saint—and she still would've hated him on principle alone. All because he did his job and he did it well. It wasn't his fault her sister's ex-husband had cheated. But it *was* his doing that Alec had walked away paying less in alimony than Elise had requested and with a hefty chunk of the Rollins' family antiques, even after his indiscretions.

"Honey, you should quit starin' and just go on and get yourself a cookie." A woman in her late sixties with burnished bronze skin and a riot of gray curls unabashedly brushed crumbs from her sweater as she sat in front of one of the many fireplaces. "I swear I'm tastin' heaven in my mouth right now."

Cole tore his eyes away from Sadie and dipped his chin in the older woman's direction. "Thanks for the suggestion, ma'am, but I don't wanna spoil my supper."

The woman waved her hand in front of her face and gestured behind him. "Nonsense! Sadie's deliciousness is definitely worth spoilin' your supper over."

He couldn't explain why those words—so sweet and innocent coming from someone older than his momma—

conjured up thoughts of him feasting on all of Sadie's *deliciousness*. He'd fall to his knees right in front of where she stood, duck his head under her flouncy red skirt, and lick up all the sweetness he had no doubt she was entirely made of.

"This nice lady's right, Cole," Edna agreed, ganging up on him. See if he offered her free legal advice the next time she put another dead animal in her ex-husband's house. "Sadie's goodies taste delicious."

"Well, go on, then," the other woman said to Sadie. "Offer this gentleman some of your goodies." With a wink, she added, "Need to do all you can to lock down a man as handsome as this one."

"Ain't that the truth?" Edna said. "Been preachin' that for years. It's our job to guide these young people, you know. Never too early to—"

As Edna prattled on about the horrors of modern dating, Cole allowed himself to drink in the sight of the woman who always seemed to throw him for a loop. She wore black leather boots up to her knees and a short red dress that twisted and twirled when she walked. Enough that a tiny voice in the back of his head prayed for a glimpse of panties any time she moved.

When he finally lifted his eyes to meet Sadie's gaze, it was full of a fire she was obviously struggling to subdue, and his lips twitched in response. What was it about this woman he was so obviously incompatible with that got him so damn hot...and hard?

"Yes," she bit out between clenched teeth, which she probably intended to be a smile. "Please. Help yourself."

The buzz of conversation between Edna and her new friend settled into background noise as he strode toward Sadie, stopping a foot from where she stood. Barring the day he'd checked in, this was as close to her as he'd ever been. Probably for the better, considering the state of his body right now. His cock always had been a disloyal bastard.

He reached out and plucked a warm cookie from the tray she held in front of her breasts—also probably for the better—and tried not to catalog the different shades of red in her hair or why those fire-spitting eyes were turning him on so fucking much. The cookies were small enough that he had no problem popping the entire thing into his mouth.

"So nice of you to savor it," she said dryly.

"Would you prefer I take this next one nice and slow?" He grabbed another cookie from the tray and bit off an exaggeratedly small bite before chewing thoroughly.

"I don't care how you take it," she said, even as she watched his lips with rapt attention.

Cole's eyebrows rose as he studied her studying him. Interesting... Apparently, he wasn't the only one feeling a bit off-balance, because, as far as he knew, she'd never before given him a second glance.

Unable to help himself from poking the bear, he leaned down, bringing their faces closer together. "I'm not sure that's true, firecracker."

His words seemed to jolt her out of her trance, and she huffed out an irritated sound, spun around, and clicked away in those wet-dream-inducing boots, taking her sweet cookies and even sweeter ass with her.

He shook his head to clear his thoughts from the delusions sleep deprivation had no doubt caused. Thanks to the change in location, he'd been running on fewer than four hours of sleep this whole week. On top of that, the coffee here wasn't the pour over espresso he usually started his day with, he hadn't been able to get his suits completely wrinkle-free after the trip over, and the mattress in his room was too soft.

He'd been living out of a suitcase for only three days, and he was already over it. He was just going to have to suck it up because he still had another three weeks of being exiled from his home while King Haven Construction renovated his kitchen and master bedroom. Eventually, he'd get used to the bed, and he'd probably start being able to function on the watered-down trash they called coffee. Based on his current circumstances, it was no wonder he'd been feeling so off-kilter.

It definitely didn't have anything to do with the gorgeous redhead shooting death glares his way like she wanted to rip him a new one...right before she ripped off his clothes.

CHAPTER 3

"Please, Sadie. I'm seriously *beggin'* for it."

Sadie stared into the pleading eyes of her cousin Natalie Haven. Her elbows were propped on the front desk, chin resting on top of her hands, folded as if in prayer.

"I don't know, Nat..."

"*Please*! You're seriously my last hope. The original couple I'd planned to photograph can't do it because they came down with the flu. And these pictures are due to this magazine *next week*."

Sadie felt bad for the situation her cousin was in, but what she was trying to pull off—photographing two random strangers as if already in a relationship—was so far out of Sadie's comfort zone, she couldn't even see the outline of her boundaries.

"You could probably find someone better suited for

this than me," Sadie said. "Maybe someone with modeling experience?"

Nat shook her head. "Nope. No. They don't *want* models. They want real people—that's the whole point of this spread. Showcasing real love with real couples across the globe."

"It sounds amazing."

"It is! I've loved shootin' these. My favorite session was this couple in Montreal. Neither of the men was very comfortable in front of the camera, but five minutes in, and they totally forgot I was there. It was just them and their love."

"But that's the thing—right now, it's just *me*. No love here."

"Let me worry about that after you say yes."

"Oh, you're so sure of my agreement, are you?" Sadie asked flatly.

"I think very highly of myself, yes, so I'm fairly certain I can get you to agree."

Sadie snorted and shook her head. "I don't know... I don't really do well in front of the camera."

Nat tipped her head back and blew out a heavy sigh toward the ceiling. "I don't know how many times I have to tell people this—*you* don't have to be good in front of a camera. *I* have to be good *behind* a camera. You let me worry about it. All you need to focus on is followin' directions—something you are excellent at, by the way. I'm always the one who screws up."

Her cousin certainly wasn't wrong. Ever since they

were little, she'd been nothing but a troublemaker, especially when she was around her two best friends.

"You do not," Sadie offered without much insistence behind it.

Nat snorted. "Don't even try that. Besides, I'm workin' on it. I'm back here, aren't I? Even though I was just home a couple weeks ago. After everything that happened with Daddy, I've been tryin' to get back more, despite the fact that I hate it here."

"How selfless of you."

"I know, right? And I planned everything like I was supposed to. I lined up a different couple than I'd originally intended so I could work this location into my schedule, but who can predict who's gonna get sick with the flu? Now, this might seriously fuck up my career, all because I wanted to come home and spend time with family..."

Oh, she was good. Sadie would give her that. She knew Nat was laying it on thick, but there was truth underneath it all. Her cousin had flown the coop at the earliest possible opportunity, and she hadn't exactly made it a priority to visit Havenbrook in the years since. It was too bad it'd taken a near tragedy to bring her back, but at least she was home—even if it was temporary. And if Sadie could make her time there a little easier to encourage her to visit more often, well...wasn't it her duty as a cousin to do so? Her aunt and Nat's mom, Caroline, deserved that. The jury was still out on Nat's daddy, Richard Haven, who was an insufferable ass even on his best days.

Sadie's shoulders slumped and Nat's eyes immediately

brightened, no doubt sensing a looming victory, but Sadie held up her hand to stop Nat's smile in its tracks. "I haven't said yes. What about your sisters? Can't you wrangle one of them into this?"

Nat huffed and rolled her eyes. "They're all pains in my ass, I swear. I could probably talk Mac into doin' it, but Hudson's stationed in Washington right now. Will said she doesn't wanna do anything in a wedding dress before her big day—like puttin' on one that's not hers is even gonna matter. And—"

"Wait, I'd have to wear a wedding dress?"

"Yes, but I promise, it's *gorgeous.*" Nat swept her newly hot-pink hair out of her eyes and continued, "And Rory's busy—something about a holiday bake sale and the girls' school. I don't know. Honestly, I don't listen too much when she talks."

Sadie laughed. "You know this would be a lot easier if you found a couple, right?"

"Uh, yeah, I do know that, actually. Unfortunately, I only know assholes who aren't interested in helpin' me. So, I'm gonna have to rely on my skill behind the camera and posin' techniques to try to get the kind of chemistry that comes from two people bein' in love."

"I think you're aimin' for a miracle. You can't fake that kind of connection."

"Let me worry about that." Nat reached for Sadie's wrist. "Look, I swear I wouldn't be askin' if it wasn't a huge deal...if I didn't really, truly need you. This spread could be career-changin' for me. It's gonna be in *the* highest-circulated wedding magazine in the country."

Sadie's mouth dropped open. "You got a spread in *Happily Ever After*?" Was it a sign that she'd just been reading the latest issue the other day?

"I did..." A slow smile spread across Nat's mouth. "You know...I was plannin' to shoot down by the covered bridge, *but*," she said, drawing out the word, "maybe we could shoot on the grounds here at the B&B. That way, we can get the inn's name in the magazine, too."

Nationwide exposure for Starlight could mean serious changes for them. As in, they'd be able to do more than just skimp by every month. Not only that, but they could hire someone to work the front desk, which would free up Elise to pursue something she actually enjoyed, and Sadie could plan more weddings—ones that would hopefully be booked thanks to this spread.

"Fine. I'll do it as long as Elise can watch the inn. But we're shootin' it here, and I want your assurance that the bed-and-breakfast will be highlighted in the piece."

Nat fist-pumped and shouted an expletive that was definitely too loud and inappropriate for the older couple currently reading in front of the fireplace. Fortunately, Mr. and Mrs. Fischer only spared them a glance before returning their attention to their afternoon activities. Two points to Sadie for spiking their hot chocolate excessively well today.

"Don't get so excited," she said. "You still have to find me a groom, right?"

Nat's shoulders sagged as she rubbed her forehead. "Yes."

"What about Nash? I know you said Rory had something goin' on with the girls, but is Nash involved in that?"

Nat barked out a laugh. "Rory'd have my ass if I even *thought* of shootin' her boyfriend with another woman, cousin or not."

Yeah, Sadie could see that. Aurora Haven, eldest Haven girl and demanding taskmaster, was definitely someone you did not want to cross.

"Honestly, what good is it havin' a local best friend if I can't exploit him for my needs?"

This time, Sadie didn't bother trying to smother her laugh. "And that other best friend of yours?"

"Asher—aka Mr. Hotshot—is on tour in Florida and scheduled to be in town in a couple weeks. And I'm not desperate enough to throw down our emergency word just to get him here early enough for the shoot. There's gotta be someone in town who could—" Nat's eyes widened as she glanced behind Sadie, a brilliant smile sweeping over her face. She fluffed her pink hair, perked up her boobs, and strode off without another word.

Before Sadie could turn to look at who'd caught Nat's attention, Mrs. Fischer walked up and plunked her empty mug on the front desk. "Oh, good, I was hoping I'd catch you," the woman said with what sounded like a Midwestern accent.

Sadie smiled. "Of course, Mrs. Fischer. What can I help you with?"

"Could you tell me a little bit about the festivities happening in town this week?"

"Yes, def—"

"Bob and I are just *so* excited to experience everything your cute little town has to offer!"

"And we're excited—"

"Do you know how we found Havenbrook?"

Having been cut off enough times, Sadie simply kept her mouth shut and smiled, raising her eyebrows in a *please continue* gesture. Sadie had no idea if it was that or the fact that the other woman seemed to have a lot to say, but she continued on.

"Well, I'm not sure if you know this," Mrs. Fischer said, leaning in as if she were about to spill a secret, "but Havenbrook is on a list of the twenty best small towns in which to spend the holidays!"

"Really?" That was just the kind of publicity they needed. Getting on a list like that could make their business boom. Especially if it was on a major site, like—

"Oh yes! On Trudy's Travel Blog. It's a little hard to read with the bright green background and white letters, but I found a ton of good information on there."

Sadie grinned, though her chest deflated slightly. Havenbrook may not be on the map for the big leagues, but at least they were getting some representation, small as it may be. "Well, I'm glad you found us, however that was. Was there something specific you were hopin' to do during your stay?"

"We just want to experience Havenbrook at this time of year in whatever way you think is best."

Sadie spent several minutes discussing with Mrs. Fischer the options that were available in town. They wanted to spread out the events over the course of their stay, so Sadie suggested a few choices for them to select from. She also made a reservation for them at the restaurant downtown that gave the best view of the huge lighted tree in the middle of the Square.

"You're such a doll. Thank you for helping us with this!" Mrs. Fischer patted Sadie's hand and squeezed before gathering up the brochures Sadie had offered and heading back to her suite, grabbing her husband from in front of the fireplace as she went.

Sadie tucked her hair behind her ear as she closed out the browser windows she'd opened to show Mrs. Fischer the offerings before remembering herself, her head snapping up as she glanced around for Nat. She did a double take when her eyes landed on her cousin. The man she was talking to had his back to Sadie, but she'd know that careless blond hair, the crisp, expensive suit, and the wide breadth of those shoulders anywhere.

"Oh, please no. No, no, no," she muttered to herself. But either there was no deity listening, or they simply didn't care to answer her prayer, because the man turned his head toward her, their eyes locking, and Sadie's stomach bottomed out.

Cole Donovan.

Nat shot her a huge grin and a wink, giving her a

thumbs-up before transitioning her hands into a completely inappropriate gesture. Sadie's face flamed, her cheeks no doubt going scarlet. As soon as Cole turned back to face Nat, her cousin dropped her hands immediately and smiled up at him.

Maybe he didn't realize who he was signing up to be posing with. Surely if he did, he wouldn't have agreed to this. As far as she could tell, their relationship, for lack of a better word, wasn't comprised of one-sided animosity.

Or...*Lord*. Maybe he intended to agree to it specifically because he knew it'd be a way to get under her skin. Hadn't this whole week he'd been staying here when he'd always managed to be in the inn at three o'clock on the dot, just in time to devour her cookies very slowly, been proof enough that he enjoyed doing that? Enjoyed torturing her?

Nat squeezed Cole's biceps and then strode directly toward Sadie, a huge grin stretching her mouth. She leaned an elbow on the front desk and turned her sparkling eyes on Sadie. "I mean, I don't want to be a dick or anything, but you should definitely be thankin' me for this. Did you *see* that man?" She waved her hand in front of her face as if she were overheated. "Holy fuck. Fortunately, he has a dark gray suit he can wear, because there's no way he could fit into the one I've been loaned. He's *got* to be packin' some serious heat, if you know what I'm sayin'."

Sadie's thoughts immediately flew to Cole's assets before she snapped her eyes shut as if that would block out the mental imagery of what he might be hiding inside his pressed suit pants. She cleared her throat. "We've, um... We've actually already met."

"Really? Great! This might not be as difficult as I thought, then."

Sadie glanced toward the dining room, finding Cole still standing there, his piercing eyes burning into her. She could never tell his emotions from simply looking at him, but by the hard set of his jaw and the tense lines of his shoulders, it was safe to say he did not look happy. Yeah, well, that made two of them.

"Actually, Nat, this might be worse."

CHAPTER 4

S adie hadn't been sure what to expect on the day of the shoot or how she'd feel. Turned out, nerves. Just straight-up nerves.

Nat had wanted to shoot in the light of the setting sun —something about the golden hour and the gorgeous glow it would cast over them. As if Sadie's anxiety leading up to the session hadn't been bad enough, now, thanks to the late session time, she'd had hours upon hours of early morning reflection today—read: anxiety daydreams—and she just wanted to get this nightmare over with.

"How much longer?" Sadie didn't even attempt to tamp down the hopeful note in her voice as she sat in a chair in front of the largest window in the room as Janine, the makeup artist, brushed and swept and dabbed various products on her.

Fortunately, the inn's honeymoon suite wasn't booked until the weekend—Naomi and her new husband having just vacated the day before—so they'd been able to commandeer it for their purposes. It was the inn's largest suite, with a bedroom, sitting room, and huge bath complete with multihead glass shower and claw-foot tub. Maybe she'd reward herself with a soak in there after this stressful day—Lord knew she'd need it. They were going to have to have the room cleaned again anyway. She might as well make the most of it.

"The majority of the women I work on usually like havin' this done, you know," Janine said with a teasing lilt.

"Yeah, well, my cousin's not most women." Nat hadn't moved from her perch next to Sadie, no doubt so she could give constant input about the hair and makeup to make sure it fit her vision.

They hadn't allowed Sadie to peer into any mirrors, so, of course, she feared the worst. She'd been sitting there for nearly three hours already—what the hell were they doing? She wasn't a vain person by nature, but she had no idea it'd take so much to make her camera-ready. She was terrified they'd turned her into someone else. Worse, what if Cole actually *liked* new, completely inauthentic her?

Better question—why did she even *care*?

"Okay, I'm just gonna apply the lashes..."

At the blob of black slowly invading her sight, Sadie jerked far enough back so Janine came into focus, said black blob pinched between the tweezers she wielded.

Sadie held up her hand. "Wait...eyelashes? I...I *have* eyelashes, though."

Nat and Janine both laughed before Janine lowered

the tweezers and rested a hand on her hip. "Relax. They come right off. Well...not *right* off because then they'd start flappin' in the breeze right in the middle of the session, but they're easy to remove. I promise."

Sadie eyed her skeptically until the other woman held up the non-tweezer-wielding hand. "Swear. I'm not even usin' the fullest option. I just wanna accentuate what you already have."

Blowing out a deep breath, Sadie nodded, even though her shoulders remained stiff. As Janine placed the eyelashes, Sadie's apprehension only grew. It felt like two caterpillars crawling on her eyelids—how could that possibly look authentic?

"How do people wear these every day?" she asked.

Janine laughed. "You'll get used to 'em."

"They're so much heavier than I thought they'd be. And are they supposed to cloud half my vision?" There was no way she remotely resembled herself. Would her twin even recognize her?

"You're gonna forget all about that when you see how hot you look," Nat said, brandishing a mirror in front of Sadie.

She froze for half a second, terrified at what she'd find, but in the end, curiosity won out. She lowered her gaze to the large mirror, and her mouth dropped open.

"Wow," she breathed.

They'd left her hair down, curled in loose waves not unlike she usually styled it, and though it felt as if she wore a pound of makeup, the effect was actually very subtle.

Deep pink stained her lips—something she wouldn't normally wear, but that she actually sort of liked—and her blue eyes popped thanks to the eye shadow colors Janine had chosen. And she'd been right. Sadie couldn't believe that the massive clump that felt like it was taking up half her vision didn't appear fake. The whole look was her, just kicked up a notch...or twelve.

Nat raised a single eyebrow. "Good 'wow,' or what the fuck 'wow'?"

Sadie huffed out a laugh and lowered the mirror, turning to catch her cousin's gaze. "Definitely good. I thought you were makin' me up to look like a totally different person."

"Why the hell would I do that? You're gorgeous. Now for the dress..." Nat's eyes brightened as she strode into the bedroom where the gown had been hanging all day.

"Have you seen it?" Sadie asked Janine as the makeup artist spritzed some sort of spray all over her face.

"Yep, and all I can say is I'd *kill* to wear a dress like that."

Well, that sounded promising at least...

Nat strolled back into the sitting room, the dress held aloft as a huge grin split her face. "*Ta-da*," she said, flipping the gown around with flourish so Sadie could see.

Sadie's smile froze as she glanced at the article of clothing she'd be wearing for the next several hours. She'd coordinated enough weddings to know the vast range of bridal gowns, so she didn't know why she'd assumed the one she'd be wearing today would be a ballgown. That was ludicrous, considering there were dozens of other styles. She now realized her assumption had been based in hope strictly out of self-preservation. Because at least a ballgown would allow for a safe distance between her and Cole. This—this full-lace dress with its plunging neckline cut clear down to damn near her belly button and see-through skirt that would tease nearly every inch of her—was *anything* but a ballgown.

"What do you think?" Nat asked. "Gorgeous, right? I'm so glad you and Anne are the same size so you could wear this one! You're gonna be stunning in it."

Sadie swallowed, the sound like a gunshot ricocheting through her head. "Will I have a shawl or anything like that?"

Nat snorted and hung the gown on the hook above the window, the light coming in behind it illustrating just how sheer the skirt was. "Course not. That'd cover all the best parts."

Yeah, it was all her *best parts* that she wanted to cover. Especially in front of Cole. At least the stylist had left her hair down, so she'd be able to use it as some sort of shield.

But as Nat helped her step into the dress, the fabric clinging to every inch of her body, the lace design concealing only her most intimate places, she knew she could've had Captain America's shield, and it still wouldn't be enough.

Sᴀᴅɪᴇ ʜᴀᴅ ʙᴇᴇɴ ʀɪɢʜᴛ. Her fears and apprehensions leading up to the shoot had materialized in front of her as soon as she stepped through the archway that led to the inn's courtyard. They'd lucked out with a warmer day, the temperature hovering in the lower fifties. Definitely colder than she usually wore sleeveless dresses in, but it could've been a lot worse.

Cole stood in front of the gazebo strung with lights and garland and surrounded by the leftover poinsettias, hand in his pocket and eyes fixed on her, looking for all the world like a gorgeous, imposing, pompous ass of a man.

Nat broke off from Sadie, walking ahead and calling out to Cole with a wave, but she couldn't pay attention to a single word her cousin spoke. Not when dormant butterflies had erupted in her stomach, fluttering around every inch inside her. Instead of listening to what were no doubt instructions from Nat, Sadie had to focus on shutting down her ridiculous body.

What the hell was she doing getting butterflies over a man like this?

It was just hormones. It had to be. Crazy, unpredictable, inconvenient hormones. She was in the middle of a long dry spell, and her body was making her pay for it now.

"All right, you two. Let's see if we can fake some chemistry," Nat said on a grin as she pulled her camera from its bag.

"I'll try to muster up some attraction," Cole said, his tone flat, not an ounce of humor to be found. He dropped his gaze to take in Sadie, and it might as well have been his lips ghosting over her skin for how her body reacted to the look.

Thank God he'd brought his jackass self with him, because his rude words were exactly what she needed to snap herself out of whatever hormone-induced stupor she'd fallen into.

She hefted up the skirt of her dress and stomped toward him as carefully as possible, her ridiculous four-inch heels needed to offset their height difference making it difficult. "You're not the only one who'll have to work on that," she snapped before turning her back to him. "You're not exactly my type."

Sadie hated to lie, but when she did, she always grounded it in as much truth as possible, hence the second part of her statement. That, certainly, was true enough. She dated nice guys. Sweet guys. *Safe* guys. Cole was none of the above.

"Okay, y'all, I'm gonna guide you how to pose," Nat said, "but I don't want you to feel boxed in, all right? If something doesn't feel natural, just move till it does. And feel free to talk while I'm shootin'. It'll be more authentic if I can catch some real smiles."

"Oh, dang," Sadie murmured, "I forgot to tell her that I don't usually smile around jackasses."

"Not even if I found all your ticklish spots?" Cole asked from behind her, the heat of his body seeping into her as goose bumps swept over her skin.

"You won't get close enough," she said, steeling her tone.

"I'm gonna need y'all to get a little closer." Nat flashed a smile. "Remember? You're supposed to be a couple. Cole, just pretend you hiked up her skirt in the dressin' room and had your wicked way with her before y'all came out here."

Sadie's mouth dropped open in shock. "Natalie Haven! I cannot believe you just said that."

With a laugh, Nat lifted a single shoulder and waved a dismissive hand. "What? Gotta break this awkward tension somehow. My dirty mind is usually the way to go."

Sadie didn't have the heart to tell her cousin it wasn't *awkward* tension that was the problem—it was just plain old tension. It'd been a constant between her and Cole since he'd first moved to town years ago. At the time, she'd actually wondered if it'd been attraction. But after they'd officially met during her sister's divorce hearings, it was clear that tension was strictly of the hate variety.

Nat was definitely going to have her work cut out for her.

"I suggested ticklin' her," Cole offered unhelpfully.

"Oh, good call!" Nat nodded, lifting her camera to her face and messing with the controls. Lowering the camera enough to meet their gazes over the top, she said, "For the record, her sides are the worst."

Sadie huffed out an indignant breath and glared daggers at her cousin. "I'm no longer speakin' to you."

"We both know that won't last."

"Don't get mad at her," Cole said to Sadie, the low

timbre of his voice rattling her insides like an earthquake. "I'm the one who brought it up."

"You'd rather I direct my irritation at you, then?"

"I don't see how that'd be different from any other day."

"Well, unlike any other day, I'm now close enough to *accidentally* inflict some bodily harm."

Cole chuckled low, the sound shocking Sadie so much, she glanced back at him, her own lips curving up without permission. But by the time she met his gaze, his lips were once again in their standard flat line, though his eyes were twinkling in a way she'd never seen.

"See?" Nat called. "Told you my dirty mind always works. Now, let's make some magic."

Nat directed them into various poses, each one more illicit than the last, and Sadie tried futilely to control her reactions. Janine hadn't needed to put on an ounce of blush for how heated Sadie had become, despite the outdoor temperature.

"Good. Now, Cole, I want you to flatten your hand on her stomach, span your fingers wide, and pull her back into you. And then just do what comes natural."

Natural? *Ha!* Sadie was stiff as a board, had been this entire time. She could feel how tight her shoulders were, practically hiked up around her ears. She just hoped it wouldn't be obvious in the pictures.

"You need to relax, or we're gonna have to do this all over again," Cole murmured. "Unless that's what you want?"

"Are you always this impossible, or just with me?"

"You do seem to bring out the best in me." He must've leaned closer, his breath now fanning over her ear and down her exposed neck, eliciting a shudder she couldn't attempt to hide. "Cold?" he asked, a cocky lilt to his voice.

"Obviously," she snapped. "You try standin' out here in fifty-degree weather, wearing barely more than Eve did."

See? Another lie rooted in reality. She *should* be cold from the temperature. But the fact of the matter was that since the moment Cole had put his hands on her, her entire body had flamed, heat burning her up from the inside. And the hard points of her nipples had absolutely nothing to do with the chill in the air.

"What can I do to warm you up, I wonder?" Cole said slowly, dipping his head to the slope where her neck met her shoulder. He ghosted his lips over the skin, and she barely held back a moan, biting her lip to keep it trapped inside where it belonged.

"Oh yes! More of this, please," Nat said excitedly, the camera shutter click-click-clicking in quick succession.

As Cole continued his subtle torture against her neck, Sadie's shoulders dipped with each second that passed, melting her body down until she had to lean back against him just to remain upright. He released a gruff sound from his throat as his grip on her stomach tightened, the hold firm and possessive. He tugged her back fully against him, the hard length of his cock pressing against her backside, and she sucked in a ragged breath as she felt him for the first time. Suddenly overwhelmingly desperate to *feel* him for the first time.

Giving herself a mental chastising, she shook herself from those thoughts. See? It wasn't just her feeling the effects of this. Her body's reaction was totally reasonable, considering this entire situation was obviously turning both their brains to mush.

"Those were so hot," Nat said, glancing down at her camera screen. "Let's do some face-to-face now that you two are warmed up."

Good. Maybe staring into the eyes of the one guy in Havenbrook she couldn't stand would be the bucket of ice water her libido needed. After seeing her flushed face, Cole wouldn't waste any time teasing her, and then they'd be back exactly where she needed them to be—at odds with each other.

But when she turned around, Cole didn't taunt or tease. Didn't ridicule or insult. Instead, he stared down at her as Nat directed them, his pale-blue eyes darker than Sadie had ever seen.

On Natalie's command, Cole wrapped one of his hands around Sadie's hip, his fingers digging into her lower back and guiding her closer so their bodies pressed tight together from the waist down. And, yep, she most definitely was not the only one still feeling the effects of this shoot. Parting his lips, he slid his other hand up her arm, over her shoulder, and to her neck, his thumb fanning against her cheek as he threaded his fingers into her hair.

Up this close, he smelled so damn good, like ocean air

41

and sunshine, and she had the absolutely ridiculous urge to press her nose to his neck and breathe him in deep. Suck him into her body and keep him there forever.

"Good," Nat said. "Now lean toward each other like you're gonna kiss..."

Thank God Cole was following directions, because Sadie was frozen, her eyes wide and anxious as she looked up at him. Cole's gaze, though, had turned heavy. Sultry. His eyes flicked from hers down to her lips and back again. They stood so close, their bodies pressed everywhere they could, and she could feel his exhales whispering across her mouth. Could taste the mint of his breath.

With one hand wrapped around his wrist, the other gripping the front of his shirt, she felt her eyes flutter closed without her permission, her lips parting as she finally gave in to this crazy chemistry between them and prepared for his kiss.

"Perfect! You guys were awesome. I think I have everything I need," Nat said, snapping Sadie out of her stupor.

She jerked back, nearly tripping over her dress's train, and Cole reached out to steady her, but she shook him off, unable to meet his eyes. "Great! Great. That's...great."

Well, that was fantastic—this whole situation had apparently zapped every ounce of her intellect so she could only say *great*. What was *not* great was that she'd very clearly lost her mind and nearly kissed Cole freaking Donovan during an extremely fictional photo shoot. She was an idiot.

"It was better than great," Nat said, stuffing her camera

and lenses into her bag. "It was amazing. Don't you think, Cole?"

Sadie refused to look at the man her cousin spoke to. The one who'd so easily blown all of Sadie's defenses out of the water, erasing three years of animosity with a single afternoon of close contact.

"Um, if we're done," Sadie interrupted before Cole could answer, "I'm freezin', so I'm gonna go on in and get changed."

Without waiting for a response, Sadie hiked up her nearly indecent dress and fled into the inn with the single ounce of dignity she had left.

CHAPTER 5

H ours later, Cole sat in the plush armchair in his
suite, looking out the window toward the gazebo on
the grounds, white lights twinkling under the pitch black
of the night sky. Remembering the feel of Sadie's curves
against him as they'd stood there, closer than they'd ever
been. He should have been embarrassed for how his body
had betrayed him, his cock growing thick and hard the
second he'd seen her walk out in that dress. But the truth
was, his reaction was nothing new. He'd been drawn to her
from the first moment he'd noticed her when he'd moved to
town, smiling brilliantly at someone in the Square. As soon
as she'd turned that grin his way, it'd knocked him on his
proverbial ass.

Their distant attraction had continued until the day
they'd officially met outside the courthouse. Recognition
had lit her gaze before realization dawned. He'd sworn he

could see her eyes shuttering right there in front of him. As he'd glanced between her and her sister—before Elise had started dyeing her hair, their appearances had been similar, though he'd never had any trouble telling them apart—he could feel her disdain practically rolling off her.

From that day on, every heated glance toward him was filled with nothing but malice and hate. And he couldn't even blame her. Cole prided himself on a job well done, and he'd lived up to that when he represented her former brother-in-law. Had done that job so well, in fact, that he'd managed to rob the very inn in which he stayed of the majority of their multigenerational family antiques. A power move on the part of his client and former fraternity brother, and something that still made Cole sick to think about.

But that was all part of the game he had to play. He got paid to make sure his clients received exactly what they wanted. Even if their intentions only came from a place of revenge. Even if it wasn't fair.

He downed the last of his bourbon before glancing at his watch. It was just before midnight, which meant the rest of the inn would be quiet and desolate. He'd found that out the second night in his temporary home. While he didn't necessarily need a lot of space, it was still quite an adjustment transitioning from a two-thousand-square-foot home all to himself, which he could roam completely naked if he so chose, to a two-hundred-square-foot box without even a kitchenette.

He stripped from his lounge pants and tugged on a pair of jeans and a hoodie, just in case he ran into any fellow guests while he was wandering around. The inn was quiet as he stepped out of his room, the hallway lit by a plethora of white lights hung from the ceiling. The bed-and-breakfast looked like St. Nick himself had thrown up inside, but Cole couldn't deny its festiveness. He could see why it was a permanent stop on the town's Sip and Shop holiday event that showcased several of Havenbrook's best.

The door directly across the hall from Cole's room opened suddenly, and Sadie stepped out, stopping short when her gaze landed on him.

"Oh!" Her hand flew to her throat as she startled. "Cole. You scared me."

He ignored the way the sound of his name on her lips shot straight to his cock. In his time staying here, he'd never seen her in the main house past nine, which was when she usually headed off to the cottage on the back of the property. Narrowing his eyes, he shifted his gaze to the door very clearly marked as the honeymoon suite.

"What're you doin' in there?" he asked. Demanded, really.

She crossed her arms over her chest and arched a single indignant brow, her face scrubbed clean of the makeup she'd worn earlier in the day and eyes so bright, he could clearly make them out even in the dim hallway. "I'm not really sure that's any of your business. Last I checked, this is *my* inn, and I don't need to account for my whereabouts to the guests."

46

Well, it was good to see the fire between them that had been stoked earlier in the day was less filled with raging attraction and now back to just rage.

"Yes, I am aware of that. Believe it or not, I did pass first grade."

"Sometimes I wonder," she mumbled just loud enough for him to hear.

He knew he shouldn't look his fill—especially after earlier. But when Sadie was around, he shifted from the detached man he'd turned himself into after his divorce to someone hungry for every ounce of her. Dropping his gaze to take her in, he followed the curve of her cheek, down her neck—lingering for only a moment where his lips had rested earlier—to the slope of her shoulder he so rarely saw. She wore a too-big holiday sweatshirt with snowmen on the front, the neckline wide and falling off one side. Her hair was pulled up, the thick mass of red waves piled on top of her head with several tendrils falling loosely around her face. Wisps of hair at her nape were damp. From sweat? He narrowed his eyes before flicking his gaze back to the door that led to the honeymoon suite, straining his ears for sounds of another person inside.

He didn't think she was seeing anyone. But then again, they weren't exactly BFFs. Hell, they weren't even acquaintances. For all he knew, she had a string of fuck buddies whom she brought back to the inn to avoid any intimate connection with her home.

"You have a gym here that I wasn't aware of?"

Sadie's brow furrowed. "What? No, why?"

47

Cole lifted his hand and ran two fingers over her damp hair, biting back his satisfaction when she shuddered at the contact. "Your hair's wet."

Sadie dropped her gaze and cleared her throat, tightening her arms over her chest, which only managed to perk up her absolutely delicious-looking breasts and made him even hungrier for her. "I'm not sure why it's any of your business, but I was utilizin' the honeymoon suite's enormous bathroom and claw-foot tub."

"Is that so?" he managed through the choke hold that vision had on him. He slid his hand into his pocket to hopefully hide the evidence of his reaction to her being naked, just across the hall from him.

"Kind of a necessity," she said, her voice oozing a fake sweetness that seemed to come so easily for her with anyone else. "See, I had this run-in earlier with a complete asshole, so I desperately needed the relaxation. Unfortunately, it looks like I might need to head right back in there as soon as we're done."

He studied her, from her full, parted lips, to her flushed chest, to the hard points of her nipples she was trying very hard to hide. One thing was clear—she may not like him very much, but she sure as hell was attracted to him. "You know what I think?"

She rolled her eyes. "Even though I don't care, I'm sure you're gonna tell me."

His lips twitched as he took a single step toward her, enough so the heat from her body radiated off her. She smelled of lavender, and he wanted nothing more than to bury his face in her neck and breathe her in. "I think that soak wasn't for relaxation at all. I think it was for relief."

She huffed out a laugh. "Relief? From what? The fact that I didn't have to be in your presence any longer?"

What would she do if he reached up and traced the neckline of that sweatshirt? If his fingertips ran perilously close to those pointed nipples taunting him... "Keep tellin' yourself that, firecracker, but you and I both know exactly what kind of tension you needed to release after earlier."

Cole didn't voice aloud that he'd needed the same. After the shoot, he'd barely managed to wait until his door had closed behind him before he'd had his pants undone and his hand wrapped tightly around his cock. Memories of Sadie's body against his had fueled his urgency as he stroked himself to completion.

Her eyes flashed with heat and hunger, the low light in the hallway illuminating the pink flush to her cheeks. She dropped her hands to her sides, and her chest rose and fell with each labored breath, the puckered tips of her breasts calling his name. "I could kick you out of the inn for sayin' something like that to me, you know."

Yeah, he knew. But even the prospect of being booted out on to the street in the middle of December wasn't enough to make him shut his mouth. He didn't know what it was about this woman, but she pushed every one of his buttons. Woke a beast inside him he hadn't even known existed until her.

"Maybe," he said, just noticing how they'd invaded each other's spaces as they'd talked, now mere inches apart. "But I think you enjoy usin' that smart mouth of yours to make my life a daily hell too much to do so."

She narrowed her eyes. "You're a complete jackass, you know that?"

"Only around you, apparently."

"Oh, that's real mature. You're blamin' me for your complete lack of manners?"

"Believe me, Sadie, the last thing I think about in your presence is manners."

"I'm sure this is gonna be good. What, exactly, do you think about while I'm around?"

He dropped his gaze to her lips, so full and pink and perfect. Ever since that first day he'd seen her in the Square, he'd wanted to know what they'd feel like. What they'd taste like. "Sometimes I wonder what you'd do if I kissed you just to shut you up."

"You...what?" Sadie's eyes flashed, her gaze falling to his mouth before snapping up to meet his again.

He cocked a single eyebrow. "Don't believe me?"

"No," she said stiffly. "I don't."

"Tell me to prove it, then," he said, his voice low and gravelly. He was done playing this game with her. Wanted to see if this tension between them exploded or fizzled out when they finally gave in to it. One way or another, he needed to move on from this woman.

"What? I'm not—"

"Tell me." This time, he gave in to the temptation to put his hands on her, sweeping his fingers over that bare shoulder, his thumb pressing lightly to the thrumming beat of her heart. "Tell me to prove it."

She stared up at him for long moments, her breathing ragged, her eyes pinning him in place. And just when he thought she'd tell him to fuck off, she whispered, "Prove it."

With a groan, he lowered his head and captured her mouth with his. She tasted of wine and chocolate, a mixture that had his cock attempting to break through his zipper after a single swipe of her tongue against his own. He moved her head how he wanted it, taking the kiss deeper as he filled his other hand with the full curve of her ass that had taunted him from afar.

She moaned as he jerked her leg up over his hip and pressed her back into the door, grinding his cock against her as the heat of her pussy seeped through their layers until it was all he could feel. All he could focus on.

He'd never been this hard in his life. Had never wanted to be inside someone more than he did right here, right now, with this woman. This woman who'd done nothing but drive him completely mad. This woman whose fingers were threaded through his hair, rocking her hips against him as they learned each other's tastes and sounds. As they—

The bell at the front desk rang at the same time Sadie's pocket buzzed, and she jerked away, stumbling in her haste to sidestep him. On instinct, Cole reached out to steady her, but she stepped out of reach, her eyes wide on him before she dropped them to the floor and spun around, walking quickly away from him and never once looking back.

CHAPTER 6

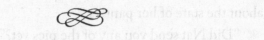

E ven though Sadie was a fully grown woman who'd had her fair share of dating disasters, she wasn't too proud to admit that she'd spent every second of every day since that kiss with Cole...hiding. There was no other way around it. She was totally hiding from him.

In her defense, she'd needed time to regroup...and also make sure she didn't turn into a puddle of goo in his presence. And it wasn't like she could go to her typical problem-solver and spill her guts about what had happened. Elise would hate her. And, yeah, okay...hate wasn't exactly a new emotion between them. You couldn't be sisters—and twins, no less—without spending a solid twenty-five percent of your time hating the other one. But the wounded look in Elise's eyes if Sadie told her she'd just had the best kiss of her life with the man who'd helped rob her sister of happiness would be even worse.

And there was absolutely no denying the power of that

kiss. It had completely and utterly eviscerated every single one that had come before. She was pretty sure her toes had actually curled as he'd swiped his tongue across hers...his hands, so hot and possessive against her, moving her body exactly how he desired. And there had been no *pretty sure* about the state of her panties.

"Did Nat send you any of the pics yet?"

Sadie jumped as her sister came up behind her, as if Elise could actually see the dirty images flipping through her mind. "What? No, why? What made you ask that?"

Elise eyed her up and down as she filled a to-go mug at their hot chocolate station, adding three scoops of peppermint flakes and five mini marshmallows, just like every day. "What's with you? I was just wonderin'."

"Oh." As inconspicuously as possible, Sadie exhaled a long, relieved breath. "No, I haven't gotten anything yet. Nat said probably today, so maybe she's already emailed." She definitely hadn't. Sadie had adjusted her notifications specifically to alert her if Nat so much as forwarded her a meme. She'd also been obsessively checking said email every five minutes just in case the aforementioned notifications weren't working.

"Text me when she does, okay?" Elise shrugged into her coat before capping her hot chocolate. "I wanna see 'em. That man may be colder than a popsicle, but there's no denyin' he's fine as hell."

Sadie ignored her sister's statement, instead focusing on what the hell she thought she was doing. "Where are you goin'?"

"Helpin' Rory with a house she's workin' on."

"What? No. C'mon, Elise. You can't keep runnin' off whenever you get an urge. It's our busiest season, and I'm drownin' over here."

Elise propped herself up on her forearms and leaned over the front desk, peeking around the computer monitor to view the schedule Sadie always had pulled up. "Looks pretty well taken care of to me."

Sadie had to bite her tongue to keep from snapping. Of course it was taken care of. Because if Sadie didn't do it, it didn't get done. She understood that Elise had been having a hard time since the divorce—even before that. Sadie had almost effortlessly fallen into her preferred profession, and Elise was still fumbling, trying to find her way. Which was why she tagged along with their cousins any chance she got, if only to feel out different careers and see if something stuck.

"It's taken care of because I made sure it was," Sadie said, her voice hard. "But that doesn't mean I don't need you here, especially to help get ready for the Olsens' wedding on Sunday."

"And I'll be back." Elise grabbed her cup and lifted it toward Sadie. "In the mornin'. Still plenty of time to get everything set up."

As she watched her sister flounce off without a backward glance, Sadie stood there, jaw locked as she stewed in frustration and resentment that had been building for a long time. Thirty-eight months, to be exact. Every day since they'd been handed the keys to the Starlight. And she was so damn sick of it.

It made her second-guess her restraint when it came to Cole. So what if her sister hated her for a little while? It wasn't like the feeling wasn't mutual at this particular point in time. And the attraction Sadie felt toward the man was hard to ignore. Actually, attraction may be too tame of a word. Her body *burned* for him, an ache so deep in her core, she wasn't even sure he could reach it—and she'd felt exactly what kind of heat he'd been packing.

Thankfully, in her world, mere attraction wasn't enough to derail her plans. With Elise bailing every chance she got, Sadie had to put all her focus on the inn. Especially with the upcoming spread in *Happily Ever After* magazine. Soon, their bookings would be through the roof, and they'd finally become the destination wedding locale she'd dreamed of since their grandma on their daddy's side had bequeathed the property to them.

Besides, it wasn't like she and Cole had anything in common other than plain old carnal lust. The local divorce attorney and the local wedding planner couldn't possibly be less compatible.

"Excuse me, dear, but would you mind telling me what holiday events in town are happening this weekend?" Mrs. Wilson, an out-of-town guest, asked.

"Not at all," Sadie said with a genuine smile, grateful for the distraction.

Of course, it was while she was tied up with Mrs. Wilson that her phone pinged with an incoming text.

Despite urgency bubbling inside her chest, she ignored it until she'd printed out a schedule highlighting the important events. But she barely waited until her guest was out of sight before she pulled her phone from her pocket and read the text from Nat.

I just emailed you some of my favorite shots. And giiiirl. They. Are. Hawt. You need to take that man for a spin if you haven't already.

Sadie's face flamed as emotions swamped her, memories of that kiss overwhelming every one of her senses. That ravenous look in Cole's eyes moments before he'd crashed his lips into hers. She could still taste him—smoky and sweet like bourbon and honey—and the scent of him had clung to her sweatshirt, even after she'd left his company.

She shook her head to rid herself of those thoughts and bit her lip as she glanced around. The majority of the guests hadn't checked in yet, so the main room was empty, and no sounds filtered in from any of the common spaces. It wouldn't hurt just to take a peek, would it?

Quickly, she navigated to her email app and looked for Natalie's name, glancing up one more time to ensure she was alone. She held her breath as she opened the message, scanning Nat's extremely brief note instructing them to let her know what they thought.

As the first image popped up on Sadie's screen, her previously held breath promptly left her in a whoosh. The picture had been taken after they'd stepped close enough that she could feel every hard inch of Cole pressing into her backside. One of his hands wrapped possessively around her hip, while his other splayed wide across her stomach, his fingers just grazing the bottom swells of her breasts as he held her tight. Her head was turned toward him, her fingers wrapped around his wrist—when had that happened?—her mouth parted as if she were waiting for a kiss. Her forehead was pressed to his temple as he bent low over her shoulder, his lips just brushing her skin, and she could tell even through the screen that she'd been breathless then just as she was now.

Each image was better—or worse, depending on how you looked at it—than the last. Not only did she and Cole look like a couple, but they looked like a couple who was insatiable for each other. A couple who was counting down the minutes until they could rip each other's clothes off and get lost in each other's bodies.

And now that she'd seen them, just how, exactly, was she supposed to pretend everything was fine the next time she ran into him? Well, she was just going to have to keep up the hiding charade, because Lord knew her panties couldn't weather another second in his presence.

SADIE HAD MANAGED to avoid Cole for a grand total of ninety minutes after cramming her eyeballs full of the might-as-well-be-indecent-for-how-hot-and-bothered-they-made-her images of the two of them.

Elise had flaked on Sadie enough times that she'd stopped taking her at her word and had just started doing stuff on her own—probably something that was ultimately only feeding Elise's irresponsibility, but that she did regardless, simply for her own peace of mind.

Which was why she was attempting to rearrange the furniture in the front gathering space all by herself. She treated every wedding held on their property as if it were her own, and that was why her brides continued referring the inn to their friends. Thank the Lord all their guests wouldn't be checking in until tomorrow at the earliest, and her grunts and groans were for her ears only. Why had she picked today of all days to wear her knee-high heeled boots and a short dress, even if it was festive?

"Magic gliders, my ass," Sadie grumbled as she attempted to lift one corner of the behemoth buffet that would house Sunday's post-wedding, pre-reception hors d'oeuvres and wine. "There's nothing magical about this."

"Need some help?" Cole's deep voice rumbled behind her.

She startled, hitting her head on the hutch on her way up. "Ow! Son of a—"

As she rubbed her hand over the tender spot at the back of her scalp, she glowered at Cole, grasping at her irritation if only to override the overpowering lust he always seemed to awaken in her. "Didn't your momma ever teach you not to sneak up on people? It's *rude*."

He dropped his gaze to where she rubbed her head before shrugging out of his suit jacket and hanging it on the coatrack by the door. "She also taught me to help if someone was in need."

After loosening his tie and hanging it with his jacket, he undid the cuffs of his dress shirt and proceeded to roll up each sleeve to just below his elbows, his eyes on her the entire time.

And damn if she didn't nearly combust.

"Wh-what are you doin'?"

Lifting a single brow, he said, "Thought that was fairly obvious."

Nope. It absolutely was not. Because she'd seen Cole do that exact move with his shirt sleeves enough times while he'd been staying there that it now starred in her fantasies. When she was alone in her room—or the honeymoon suite's tub, as it were—and she inevitably conjured up his image in her mind, it was this, exactly. Those eyes boring into hers as he made quick work of his shirt sleeves before cupping her ass in his large hands, tossing her on a bed, and burying his face between her thighs.

"Sadie?"

She snapped her eyes to his, ignoring how her breath had suddenly become more labored and her cheeks warmed at the memory of her fantasies. "Um, what?"

He raised a brow. "Where do you want it?"

"'scuse me?" she squeaked, heart pounding like a bass drum in her ears.

He studied her for long moments, his gaze seeming to read into every twitch and shift she made. Cataloging.

Calculating. Finally, he said, "The piece of furniture. Where do you want it?"

"Oh, right. Of course." She straightened and brushed a hand down the front of her dark green velvet dress, attempting to collect herself even though her brain had boarded the runaway express to Trouble Central. "Ideally, over there," she said, pointing to the east wall. "If you can move it that far."

Cole ran a hand down the whisper of scruff along his jaw and shook his head. "Do you have trouble sleepin' each night if you don't get in your quota of insults?"

She played back her words and cringed, for once not meaning them as they'd come out. She held up her hands. "Believe it or not, I didn't intend for that to be an insult."

"Then you're on your game more than usual tonight."

Breathing out a laugh, she shook her head and glanced at the floor, unable to meet his gaze as flashes of their images flipped through her mind. Ever since she'd opened that email, had borne witness to the chemistry she and Cole so very obviously shared, she'd been so far off her game it wasn't even funny. "I am definitely not that."

He only offered her a grunt of acknowledgment as he squatted down and lifted a corner of the buffet without strain, sliding one of the round magic gliders under the wood. "You always dress like that for manual labor?"

She glanced down at herself, feeling stupid all over again. She had no idea why she'd worn this today, considering she'd known she'd have to prep the inn for the wedding—and do it all, more than likely, by herself. No, that was a lie. She totally knew why she'd worn this. Because the rich emerald green set off her complexion, and she'd received enough compliments on it paired with the boots that she knew it was a killer outfit. A *date* outfit.

Except the Starlight wasn't a date locale.

Nope, she'd worn this with the sole intention of catching Cole's eye, should they happen to cross paths. Had been doing the same thing all week, despite hiding from him as best she could.

"Not my smartest choice," she finally admitted.

Cole didn't respond as he made quick work of the other gliders, placing them into position before standing to his full height and turning the weight of his gaze on her. He drank her in, his eyes sweeping over her body so viscerally she felt it straight to her core.

"I wouldn't say that," he murmured before turning away from her and easily moving the piece where she'd instructed.

Once it was situated in place, he removed the gliders from beneath it and handed her the stack of them.

"Thank you." It was, quite possibly, the first nice thing she'd ever said to him, and how sad was that? After all, her anger toward this man stemmed entirely from the loyalty she had toward her sister, who didn't seem to return the sentiment.

"Why're you tryin' to do this all by yourself anyway?" He held up a hand and stopped her when she'd opened her mouth to snap back at him. "I'm not sayin' you can't, just that it'd be a lot easier with two of you."

Sadie lifted a shoulder as they strolled back into the great room. "Elise helps me"—*rarely*—"but she ducked out early."

He hummed in acknowledgment. "I see. I suppose that means you haven't had a chance to look at the email Nat sent."

She rolled her lips between her teeth and quickly diverted her gaze, focusing everywhere but on him. If she met his eyes...well, she had no idea what would happen. She may spontaneously combust—Lord knew it was hot enough between them that it wasn't completely out of the realm of possibility.

"No, I didn't," she said, willing her voice not to shake as she lied her ass off—a new habit she'd picked up while in his presence. She stepped behind the front desk and focused on the computer, closing down each program for the day since it was nearing nine.

"Really." His tone was flat, disbelieving, and that only sparked her irritation.

"Yes, really," she snapped. "Is that so hard to believe? Can't imagine a woman not trippin' over herself just for a glimpse of you on her screen?"

"Trippin' over herself, huh? You speakin' from experience?"

"Absolutely not," she said stiffly, ignoring Cole's close proximity as she exited out of their calendar app...realizing too late that she'd pulled up the email on the desktop to see the images on a larger screen. And there they were, for all the world—or at least Cole—to see. The one currently showcased was after they'd turned to face each other, his hands cupping her cheeks and hers fisted in the front of his shirt, their lips a mere breath apart.

He stepped into the tight space behind her and braced his hands on the desk on either side of her hips, leaning forward until the length of his body pressed against every one of her curves. "You might wanna call someone about this. Looks like you've been hacked," he said into her ear, his voice nothing more than a low rumble.

Oh, sweet baby Jesus, she didn't have enough willpower to resist this man. It was one thing when she'd hated him silently from afar before they'd ever had a conversation. But this...this push and pull with him was getting to be too much, turning her brain to ash.

"Or maybe..." he continued, "you thought these were just as fucking hot as I did, and you spent all afternoon forcin' yourself not to look at 'em again. And again. And again." He punctuated each sentence with a sweep of his lips against the side of her neck, and she had to grip the counter just to keep herself upright.

Her breaths sawed in and out of her, her nipples tight and peaked, her pussy so wet, he could bend her over right there and slide inside with ease. Fill her completely and steal her breath once and for all.

"So, which is it, firecracker? You can tell me that someone hacked your account and pulled up this email, I'll head to my room, and we won't ever have to talk about this again."

Heaven help her, but she couldn't stop the single word from leaving her lips. "Or?"

He splayed a hand across her abdomen, nearly identical to how it'd been during the photo shoot, and pulled her back against him, ensuring she knew exactly how invested he was in her answer. "Or we see if the chemistry between us is just as potent in the bedroom as it is outside of it."

CHAPTER 7

ole was either about to get a knee to his groin or have the best sex of his life. There was no in-between, no middle ground. There never was when it came to Sadie.

She was quiet so long, her body frozen in front of him, that he feared he'd read the situation all wrong and his balls were about to pay the price for that error.

But then she dropped her head forward, her fingers curling over the edge of the front desk, and she breathed out a simple plea. "Or."

That single word might as well have been a shotgun for how Cole sprang into action, gripping her hips and spinning her around to face him, not even waiting until she'd gotten her bearings before cupping her face and crashing his lips down on hers. He groaned as she allowed him entry into her mouth, reveling in her sweetness, subtle hints of chocolate and peppermint on her tongue as she teased him. Before the night was through, he hoped to God he'd get to find out where else she tasted as sweet.

He dropped a hand to her thigh, trailing his fingers along her soft skin and not stopping until he encountered the lace hem of her panties against her ass. With a groan, he gripped a handful of her lush curves and lifted her up against him, encouraging her to wrap her legs around his waist. Desperate to get her closer, to hear her soft whimper when he nipped her bottom lip just like she'd done the other night. Sadie complied without hesitation, the skirt of her dress bunching around her hips and allowing the full heat of her lace-covered pussy to taunt his cock.

"Sadie..." he said against her mouth, barely able to pull back enough to whisper her name. Christ, he couldn't get enough of this woman. Hadn't been able to stop thinking about their first kiss since it'd happened. She drove him out of his mind most days, but since their midnight encounter, it had become damn near painful to be in the same vicinity as her and not have her lips against his, her curves filling his hands, her scent in his lungs.

She whimpered, tightened her legs, and ground down even harder against him. He had no idea how she managed to completely eviscerate his self-control—something he prided himself on, but which he was woefully lacking while in her presence—but he probably should've been more concerned about what that meant than he was.

While he'd love nothing more than to fuck her right

there in the open, possible audience be damned, he figured the other guests might frown upon that, and he didn't want to damage Sadie's reputation within her own establishment.

He forced himself to pull away, an astonishing feat considering how tightly she was wrapped around him, her fingers threaded through his hair and her lips hot and urgent against his. "My room?"

"Yes," she said, without an ounce of hesitation, her tone breathless and urgent.

Her confident response only fueled the fire already raging inside him, licking against his skin. He couldn't bring himself to pull his mouth from hers for even a second as he guided them down the hall to his guest suite. Fumbling blindly with the keypad on his door, he swore against her lips until it finally unlocked after the third try.

"I hope you're better in bed than you were at unlockin' that door." She cupped his neck, holding him in place as she nipped his ear, the taunt laced with a playful edge she hadn't used with him before.

He ignored how much he liked it...how much he liked *her* despite everything. But this was just sex. It had to be. The two of them didn't make sense. Sadie had forever in her sights, and Cole had already been there, done that, had the monthly alimony payments to prove it.

"You're gonna pay for that." Cole squeezed her ass, kneading the flesh and grinding her down harder against him.

She broke away on a gasp, her head tossed back as she moaned. "Cole..."

"Fuck," he whispered under his breath, looking his fill. From her closed eyes to her parted lips to her breasts pushed up and just begging for his mouth, this gorgeous woman drove him absolutely crazy. She consistently challenged him, kept him on his toes, and he'd never wanted someone more. "Say it again."

She lowered her gaze to his, her eyes heavy, lip caught between her teeth. "Make me."

"Oh, I intend to." He tossed her onto the bed and braced himself on his arms above her. "I'm gonna make you cry it out again and again and again. Gonna make your throat hoarse from screamin' it."

She slid her hands over his shoulders, locking her fingers together behind his neck, the spark in her eyes telling him she wanted to play. "You're awfully cocky considerin' we both still have all our clothes on. How about we start with the first one and go from there?"

He lowered himself until his mouth hovered just above hers and her breath whispered against his lips. "It's not cocky if you're certain. And I'm one hundred percent certain I'm gonna make this pussy throb for me twice before I even slide my cock inside."

Sadie's eyes widened, her breaths growing faster as she stared up at him. Christ, she was a sight, hair like fire spilling out over the white sheets, the dress she wore showcasing each and every mouthwatering curve. Those goddamn boots teased him within an inch of his life, and the tiny glimpse of red lace between her thighs finished him off.

He pushed back and stood without giving in to the kiss they both obviously wanted, working on the buttons of his shirt. "Strip for me," he managed through a throat made up entirely of gravel.

There'd been so much fire between them, he needed to know she was in this without a doubt. Even though she'd said yes to Cole bringing her to his room, he wanted to be absolutely certain she still wanted this.

Without pause, she sat up, gripped the hem of her dress, and tore it over her head in one fluid motion. And then, wearing nothing but those tiny red lace panties and matching bra, she leaned back on her arms, presenting herself to him on the bed in which he'd fantasized about her, stroking himself to thoughts of her and nothing more. Her breasts spilled out over the top of her low-cut bra, the dusky edges of her nipples peeking out to tease, and he couldn't wait another second before he got a taste.

"Fuck, you're so gorgeous." He braced his hands on either side of her hips and engulfed one peaked nipple into his mouth, lace and all.

Gasping, she threaded her fingers through his hair and took him with her as she fell back against the bed, his name another groan on her lips.

"Told you." He peeled down the cup of her bra before swiping his tongue over the puckered tip and sucking it deep.

"You told me you'd make me come twice," she said as

she squirmed against him. "Believe me, it hasn't happened yet."

Slowly, with purpose, he lifted his eyes to her as he swiped his tongue over her nipple, then drew back and blew against it. He refused to smile as she shuddered in response, lifting up her hips as if seeking friction. "I should hope not. I haven't even touched your pussy yet."

She huffed out a breath when he kept the strokes of his cock light against her. "Yeah, I noticed. Performance anxiety?" she asked with mock concern.

If he weren't so impressed by her acting ability, he would've laughed at her ridiculous statement. There was no denying his very obvious erection nestled in the warm valley between her thighs. No denying how she continued to attempt to work herself against it, either.

"I don't suppose you have a ball gag anywhere around here, do you?"

She breathed out a laugh, her eyes flickering in surprise and something else—delight?—as she shoved at his chest. "No ball gags," she said firmly, brooking no argument. "Because Lord knows you'd never stop runnin' your mouth even if you robbed me of the ability to use mine."

Well, she had him there. After seeing her nearly naked, watching how she responded to him before he'd even really, truly begun, there was no way he could keep quiet while he savored her. And he intended to spend the entire night savoring every single inch.

Instead of revealing that, he raised an eyebrow and slid down her body, brushing his lips against her petal-soft skin along the way. "Guess I'll have to find another way to shut you up, then."

"I'm not sure how you're gonna do that," she said as he peeled her panties down her legs and feasted on the sight of her, so pink and glistening. Mouthwatering. Perfect. "Especially when you're so infuriatin' that I have to keep—"

At the first swipe of his tongue against her, she broke off as her moan tore through the room. Fuck, he knew she'd be sweet. Knew he wouldn't be able to get enough of her once he had his first taste, but he'd have to figure that shit out because they were destined for only a single night. He was hard as a rock, his erection throbbing and angry, demanding release as he flicked his tongue against Sadie and slid two fingers inside the heaven he couldn't wait to feel surrounding his cock.

She groaned and arched against his mouth, grinding her clit harder as she gripped his hair and held him tightly to her. He doubled down, pride swelling in his chest that she was already so close when he hadn't even really gotten started. Increasing his pressure and speed, he didn't let up until her pussy fluttered around his fingers.

"Let me hear it," he murmured against her, teasing his lower lip over her swollen clit.

"Shut—"

Sucking her hard into his mouth, he reveled in her surprised gasp and how her body responded to him. He didn't bother to suppress his satisfied smirk as she arched up and came around his fingers, his name a long, low moan falling from her lips.

Collapsing back on the bed, she loosened her fingers in his hair and massaged his scalp as if in apology for her rough handling. As if she'd forgotten herself for a moment and had gotten wrapped up in sensation, too lost in what he was provoking in her to pay attention to niceties.

He liked that far more than he should've, but he'd be lying if he said that wasn't exactly how he wanted her tonight. Ragged and wild and frenzied. Everything she'd managed to stoke in him without even trying. Everything he'd never allow to show.

He placed a single kiss to her clit and another on the inside of her thigh before he climbed up her body. Braced on his hands above her, he stared down into her face, cataloging the rise and fall of her chest, the flush to her cheeks, the desire swimming in her eyes, and tried to tamp down the satisfaction flooding his body.

"What's that look for?" she asked, narrowing her eyes as she poked a finger into his chest. "I could've sworn you promised me two."

Unaware he'd been smiling, he wiped it clean off his face and nodded slowly. "I do seem to recall that, yes."

"I can always help you out if you don't think you'll be able to hold up your end of the bargain." She slid her hand over her breast and down her stomach, her intent clear.

Settling on his side next to her, he brushed her hand away before she could reach her destination. "Next time, you can fuck yourself with your fingers, and I'll happily watch. But tonight, this is mine."

She seemed to startle at his words, but as fast as the look appeared, it vanished, her eyes turning hazy as Cole cupped her.

He glided his fingers between her pussy lips, groaning at the slick glide of skin on skin. "Fuck, you're so goddamn wet."

She whimpered in response, and he couldn't deny how pride swelled in his chest at stealing her words. Turning her incoherent, if only for a short while. With each stroke of his fingers, he studied her reactions, reveling in every sharp intake of breath, every panted gasp, every arch of her hips.

As soon as she slid her hands up her stomach to her breasts, pulling down the other bra cup so she could play with both nipples, he couldn't hold himself back any longer. He lowered his head and sucked her nipple into his mouth at the same time he sank two fingers inside her.

She breathed out a moan and lifted her breast for him. "*Oh*—just like that. Please, don't stop."

He groaned as her walls contracted around his pumping fingers, fearing he'd become addicted to this woman. To the feel of her body against his and his name on her lips. To the scent of her on his sheets and his body. To how, in her presence, he felt alive for the first time in years.

"I've thought about this a hundred different ways," he admitted into her skin, her pleasure a drug making him loose-lipped. "But even my dirty imagination didn't do this perfect pussy justice. Can't wait to be inside you. Can't wait to—"

"*Cole*." She tossed her head back and whimpered toward the ceiling, rolling her hips as she came for the second time.

He lightened the pressure of his palm against her clit as he continued to pump his fingers into her, extending her pleasure as long as possible. And as much as he'd loved hearing her cry his name once again, it had nothing on the look she pinned him with—one filled with desperation and need. With desire and want and an urgency he wholly and completely reciprocated.

For half a second, he considered telling her to strip the rest of the way, but the sight of her there, her tits spilling out over the top of her bra and the black leather of her boots so stark against the creaminess of her skin, would fuel his fantasies for the foreseeable future. He had no intention of robbing himself of that, especially considering this might be—*needed* to be—his only night with her.

Standing, he shrugged out of his shirt and tossed it aside before ridding himself of his suit pants and boxer briefs. He'd waited long enough to be inside her—years, if you wanted to get right down to the truth. He didn't intend to wait a second more.

After sheathing himself with a condom from his wallet, he gripped her thighs and yanked her to the edge of the bed until her ass hung just off the side. "I think you owe me a couple more."

"Orgasms?" she asked incredulously. "You're good

with your hands and mouth, I'll give you that. But makin' me come durin' sex takes a lot more than just a big dick."

He raised an eyebrow. "You think I have a big dick? That's the nicest thing you've ever said to me." He swiped his cock through the slickness of her pussy, taunting them both.

"It wasn't a compliment. Merely an observation. You've got average beat by a few inches. Can't argue with facts," she said, her breath stuttering when he flicked the head of his cock across her clit.

"I see. And what about the part where you said I'm good with my hands and mouth?"

"I— Well—"

"Speechless," he said, shaking his head. "Never thought I'd see the day."

She wrapped her legs around his waist, digging the heels of her boots into his ass. "Were you plannin' on talkin' me to orgasm? If so, you might wanna reconsider your approach."

"Oh, firecracker, I think we both know just how much you *love* my approach." He slid his cock through her slick pussy lips, barely holding back a groan at the easy glide her wetness provided. "I told you I'd make this pussy throb for me, didn't I? And I was right. Just never knew how wet I could get it. Had no idea you'd soak my cock."

She parted her lips, no doubt to mouth off, but he took that opportunity to slide inside her, the tightness nearly robbing him of breath. His eyes rolled back as he got lost in the heaven between her legs, and he wasn't even fully seated yet.

Remembering himself and that he didn't want to miss a second of her reactions, he glanced down at her, their gazes connecting as he continued slowly filling her. Her eyes widened with each inch he slid inside, her nails biting into his forearms as her mouth fell open in a silent plea.

"*Christ*, Sadie."

As soon as his hips sat flush against hers, he realized his error. Not only was one night not going to be nearly enough, but if he lasted long enough to get her off, he deserved a fucking medal. As it was, he'd be lucky if he didn't explode after ten strokes.

She exhaled his name, her fingers curling around his neck as she tugged him down to her, her lips hungry and demanding. He kissed her, thankful for the chance to get himself together. Except there was no getting himself together when it came to Sadie. Everything she did drove him out of his mind, including kissing. Especially when she started rocking her hips up toward him, grinding her clit against the base of his cock.

With a groan, he pulled his hips back and snapped them forward, plunging inside her over and over again. The movement was so jarring, they merely rested their opened mouths against each other, exchanging breaths and moans, as he drove them both toward ecstasy.

Desperate to feel her come around him, he gripped her leg and hiked it up over his hip, grinding hard against her on each downstroke. Her breaths came faster, her fingers tightening against him right along with her pussy.

"I'm—" As soon as she sobbed out a breath, her eyes locked on him as she squeezed his cock, he finally allowed himself to let go, at her mercy as she dragged him over the edge.

In more ways than one.

CHAPTER 8

Sadie might've gone to sleep in her own bed, alone, but for all that she'd dreamed about Cole, he might as well have been next to her the entire night. She'd felt his lips on her shoulders, her neck, her breasts... Remembered the tight grip of his hands on her hips as he pumped inside her, his fingers delving into her hair, his breath ghosting across her lips.

She'd woken up wet and wanting, frustration heavy in her limbs over what she wouldn't be having today...or anytime soon. She should've seen it coming, but after she'd left Cole's room last night, blissed-out and completely sated, worrying over nothing more than if her jellylike legs would be able to carry her to the guest house, she hadn't thought much about what the next day would bring.

And now she was just supposed to go on like business as usual?

She didn't know how that was possible, what since he was

living in her inn for the foreseeable future. And what since she hadn't managed to go more than three minutes all day without recalling a particular moment from the night before—like how the scruff of his jaw felt on her inner thighs, or the smug sparkle in his eyes when he'd blown across her wet nipple, or the sound of her name falling from his lips as he'd lost himself inside her.

So, yeah. Operation Get Cole Out of Her System was going just *great*.

And of course, because her luck was her luck, it was a Saturday, which meant he hadn't even escaped to the office. Instead, he'd reserved the conference room all day and had spent the entirety of it driving her mad. She'd watched him go in and out all morning, and each time he'd done so, his gaze would lock on hers without hesitation, and she'd lose her breath. It was beginning to feel a little like she was losing her mind too.

Last night, when he'd been inside her, she hadn't had any problem reading his eyes. Now, though... Now, she had no idea what was going through that gorgeous head of his. No idea if he was regretting what had happened between them and cursing the fact that he was staying at Starlight, or if he, like her, had been replaying it every chance he got.

Had he woken up hard to thoughts of her?

"What's got your attention today?"

Sadie jumped at the sound of her sister's voice and pressed a hand to her chest to calm her racing heart. "*Elise*... You scared me."

"Clearly." Elise raised an eyebrow and then glanced over her shoulder to the now-closed conference room door where Sadie had been staring the better part of the morning. "Daydreaming on the job, huh?"

"What?" she squeaked. "No. Why would you say that? Of course not."

Elise snorted and fixed herself her morning cup of hot chocolate, focusing on the task and luckily not on Sadie's reddening cheeks. "I said it because I could practically see the drool hanging off the corners of your mouth when I came over."

Sadie sputtered but couldn't manage to find any words to argue that statement. Mostly because she'd never been very good at lying to her sister, so there was no reason for her to believe she'd be able to start now. But she absolutely could not tell Elise that she'd welcomed her sister's ex-husband's divorce attorney into her bed last night. Absolutely *would* not tell her sister it had been the best sex of her life.

"Don't look so scandalized." Elise waved a hand as she scooped marshmallows into her cup. "It's not like you're the only one. Pretty sure Mr. Cold as Ice is frequent fantasy fodder for every person in Havenbrook who swings that way—and maybe even some who don't."

Before Sadie could rebuke her, the front door opened and in swept Edna wearing a bright-red holiday sweater that could probably be seen from space.

"Mornin', girls," she said, dropping today's mail into

their bin and gathering the few pieces they had going out. "What kind of gossip have y'all got for me today?"

Elise blew into her to-go mug—because, of course, she wasn't planning on sticking around. Why would she when Sadie was barely treading water, and they had a wedding tomorrow to prep for?—and met Sadie's eyes over the rim, a gleam in hers. "We were just chattin' about how delectable Cole is. Sadie's got a bit of a crush, I think."

Sadie's jaw dropped, and she stared at her sister in horror. "*Elise.*" Then, turning to Edna, she said, "She's just tryin' to get under my skin is all. We were talkin' about... Um... The traditional German holiday cookies I'll be makin' for Monday's bakin' class! Just like our grandma used to bake every year."

Edna's gaze was as sharp as ever, no doubt seeing more in Sadie's expression than she intended. A sly grin swept over her face, and she winked. "Well, both those things sound absolutely delicious. And, Elise, you're right. Cole is most definitely in the spank bank for nearly all of Havenbrook."

Sadie's mouth dropped open as she huffed out a disbelieving laugh and watched as the older woman speed-walked her way out of the inn, the bells on her sweater jingling as she went.

With narrowed eyes, Sadie spun on her sister. "You're the actual devil, do you know that?"

Elise just laughed and put the lid on her cup before heading toward the coatrack. But Sadie wasn't having any of that, and certainly not now after Elise had thrown her under the bus without a second thought. It was time her sister started pulling her weight a little bit around here, and it was time Sadie stopped enabling her.

"Don't even think about it," Sadie snapped. "I'm leavin', and you're watchin' the inn and makin' sure the honeymoon suite is up to the specifications the bride has requested. It's the least you can do after that mortifying —*completely fabricated*—tale."

"But I—"

Sadie raised her hand, dismissing her sister's words. "Don't care. I'm takin' a lunch and then runnin' a few errands to get supplies for the Bake with Me session on Monday. I'll be back later. Try not to burn the place down."

Without another word, Sadie grabbed her coat and purse and headed out into the crisp December air with absolutely no destination in mind. It didn't matter that she'd left her sister in charge of the inn and of a bride's happiness. All she could think about was that maybe if she had some time away from Cole, that would help get him out of her head...

Turned out, it didn't matter how long Sadie had spent away from the inn. Apparently, it wasn't her proximity to Cole that had her hormones in overdrive, because she managed to get herself worked up while she was out and about in town with nothing more than a glance at the eggplants in the grocery store. Honestly, what was the matter with her?

She didn't make it back to Starlight until the early evening—late enough to royally piss off her sister—but there was a method to her madness. If she waited long enough, maybe Cole would be finished in the conference room and already tucked away in his suite for the evening.

Soft holiday music played from the Bluetooth speakers at the front desk, and a fire crackled in the parlor's fireplace as Sadie made her way through the inn. She greeted a couple of the guests who milled about, while her body was on high alert for any Cole sighting. A quick glance around proved promising. The door to the conference room was open, the interior dark, and there was no tall, blond, and brooding man lingering as far as the eye could see. She exhaled a quick sigh of relief, ignoring the sudden and unexpected wave of disappointment that hit her. Honestly, what did she have to be disappointed about?

"You didn't tell me you'd be gone all afternoon," Elise said with a glare as she rounded the front desk.

Her arms laden with grocery bags, Sadie rolled her eyes. "Yeah, it really sucks when someone bails on you without notice, doesn't it?"

"Whatever. You're on call for the rest of the night."

"So what else is new?"

With a huff of irritation, Elise swept past Sadie, grabbed her coat from the rack, and disappeared out the front door with nothing more than a wave—or was that a one-fingered salute? Yeah, her *sister* was the one who deserved to get huffy. This passive-aggressiveness between them wouldn't hold up for much longer. If the past was any indication, it'd only be another couple weeks, tops, before they'd come to blows.

She could worry about that later. Right now, she already had enough on her plate to keep her mind occupied since she was clearly on her own for the rest of the night. She just hoped Cole didn't make an appearance, because she had no idea what she'd say to him if he did.

Was it appropriate to tell your one-night stand that you'd fantasized about him and all he could do with his tongue and fingers—not to mention the way-larger-than-average appendage he wielded like a professional? She wasn't overly knowledgeable about this side of dating, but she doubted that was something that should be done. So then, was she just supposed to ignore him? Pretend nothing had happened between them? Acknowledge it had, but pretend it hadn't been the best of her life? That she didn't want to do it a dozen more times? And then maybe a dozen more after that just for the hell of it?

Honestly, there should be a handbook for this. How else could single women know what was appropriate interaction with their one-night stand?

After verifying the guests in the common spaces didn't currently need anything, she headed to the kitchen to put away the groceries she'd purchased for the baking class later in the week. She dropped the bags on the large island in the middle of the room and went to work putting away everything. She was so focused on the task—anything to take her mind off a certain someone—that she didn't realize she wasn't alone until she spun around, her arms laden with almond flour, sugar, and cinnamon, and ran straight into a wall of warm, male flesh. Warm, *hard,* male flesh.

She yelped and scrambled to keep hold of everything while Cole reached out to steady her, his hands enveloping her shoulders, the weight of them comforting in a way she didn't want to think about.

"Easy," he said, his voice just a low murmur. A murmur she was now intimately acquainted with. He swept his thumbs down over her collarbone, and she had to bite her lip to stifle a moan. "I was beginning to think I'd run you off."

Clutching the items to her chest, she scoffed and made herself meet his eyes before darting them away and focusing on the items in her arms. "You think an awful lot of yourself, don't you? Believe it or not, I didn't plan my day around you."

Not her *whole* day, anyway. Just the majority of it.

Cole hummed low in his throat. "Well, that makes one of us."

She snapped her gaze up to his, but he wasn't looking at her. Instead, he focused on the items in her arms and took them from her grasp.

"Need some help?" he asked, without waiting for an answer.

"I...um—" She shook her head as she watched him walk straight for the open pantry door...and put each thing in the wrong spot.

With a sigh, she followed behind and pushed him to the side of the walk-in pantry, grabbing the almond flour from where he'd set it and shifting it down two shelves and to the left. "I should've known you'd try to elbow your way into something as simple as putting away groceries. Honestly, don't you think it'd be smarter to just ask where they go instead of assumin' you know everything, like a jackass?"

Standing on tiptoes, she reached up and grabbed the sugar he'd placed on the highest shelf, irritated that he hadn't just asked her where it went in the first place. Sometime in the second and a half it'd taken her to grab the item, Cole had stepped up behind her. So close, her back slid down his front as she settled her feet back on the floor. She froze as he wrapped his fingers around her hip, the scent of his shampoo filling her senses as he leaned his head down close to hers.

"But if I did that, I wouldn't have gotten you in here with me." His breath ghosted over her shoulder and neck, tightening her nipples into stiff, traitorous peaks.

Still facing away, she bit her lip, her eyes fluttering closed as she allowed herself just to feel the solid weight of him behind her. "That desperate for a lesson in organization, huh?" she managed through a tight throat.

"I'm desperate, but not for that." He reached around, plucked the bag of sugar out of her hand, and placed it in the exact right spot. Then he flattened his hand on her stomach and tugged her back into him so she could feel just exactly how desperate he was.

"We never said what this was." Cole's lips brushed the shell of her ear with every word, and she had no hope at all of holding in a shudder. "If last night was enough for you, you can tell me to fuck off, and I'll leave."

She licked her lips and forced herself to stand still. To not lean back into him or grip his hand and drag it higher... or lower. "Or?"

He breathed out a laugh, sweeping his lips up and down the length of her neck. "That's how you wanna play it again, huh? Fine. *Or* I'll pull this door shut and fuck you up against it. Up to you, firecracker, as always."

Was there even a question? Apparently, yes. Her body was screaming at her to say "Or." *Or, or, or.* But her brain... her brain was wondering what the hell she thought she was doing. Was worried about the ramifications of this. A one-night stand was one thing, but twice was something else entirely. And if they went down this path of a repeat, who was to say they would stop after tonight?

Turned out it didn't matter what objections her brain came up with, because her body was in control of this situation. She reached behind her and cupped Cole through his jeans, feeling the hard length of him throb in her hand. She gave his cock a squeeze, bit her lip, and settled her back against his chest. "I'm afraid I'm startin' to be predictable around you."

Cole moaned low in his throat as she rubbed him through his pants. "You're anything but that. And even if you were, I'm definitely not complainin'."

"You're also not doin' anything. Thought you said

something about an intention you had once you got me in here..."

Cole sank his teeth into her skin where her neck met her shoulder, and her clit throbbed from the contact. Lord, he hadn't even really touched her and she was already panting and on edge—hell, she had been all day. Had been since she'd woken up with her legs tangled in her sheets and her panties an absolute mess. All thanks to the infuriating, button-pushing, insanely hot man at her back.

"You should know from last night that I always deliver what I promise." He reached back and pulled the door closed behind them, plunging them into darkness.

Though she couldn't see Cole, she could feel him. Could sense him, somehow, as he came closer, her body humming at the promise of what was to come.

"Workin' in the conference room today was the biggest mistake I could've made," he said, his voice a low rumble as he grabbed her by the hips and turned her to face him.

She swallowed hard and did her best to ignore the soft strokes of his fingers along the low scooped neckline of her dress. "Why's that?"

"Because instead of focusin' on strategy for upcoming cases, I was remembering what it felt like to be inside you. Couldn't think about anything else all fucking day. I thought about the sweetness of your pussy...how you'd moan my name all breathy when you were about to come..."

"I did not."

He huffed out a laugh. "You did, and you know it.

Don't make me prove it again right now. Who knows when someone'll come lookin' for you. Would hate to have them hear you gettin' fucked right up against this door where you make their beloved afternoon cookies."

Oh Lord... There *were* guests just a few feet away in the parlor, and who knew where the others were. It was still early enough that they definitely weren't in for the night. It was entirely plausible—probable, even—that they'd wander around, intent on finding her. On asking a question or getting a recommendation. And she was hiding in the kitchen pantry about to be fucked by a man she had no business being involved with in the first place.

And, God help her, but the entire situation only made her hotter.

Heat engulfed her a second before Cole's hands settled on her, sliding up over her waist until he cupped her breasts, his thumbs brushing over the hard peaks.

He chuckled under his breath, tucking his head into the crook of her neck as he reached around and palmed her ass. "Should've known my firecracker would like that idea. You want them to know how hot you get 'cause of me?"

"I don't—"

"Or maybe you want them to know how wet I make you?" He inched his hands under her dress, dancing his fingertips up her bare thighs until he came in contact with the lace panties she maybe-definitely put on this morning with this very thing in mind.

"I'm not—"

"Or just how much you love bein' stuffed full of my

cock? Your sweet little pussy stretchin' to take every inch of me..." He tucked his fingers beneath the material and squeezed her ass before moving his hand around to the front and slipping his thumb between her skin and the fabric, sweeping the digit across her aching pussy.

She caught a moan in her throat before it managed to escape, but her knees were definitely in jeopardy of buckling. She gripped his biceps just to hold herself up, though that didn't do anything but remind her with every flex of muscle just exactly what he was doing with his hands. "I—"

"Tell me every word of what I said isn't true." His fingers joined his thumb and swept through her wetness, all of them working in tandem to drive her out of her mind. "Tell me this pussy isn't needy for me. I'm waitin'."

Her eyes rolled back when he pinched her clit between his thumb and forefinger, rubbing on either side to the point of madness. Honestly, she might as well be Niagara Falls for as wet as she was, and she wasn't interested in this game of cat and mouse. He'd already caught her—she'd *let* him. And now she wanted the fun that came with that.

"I'm waitin' too," she said, tugging on the button of his jeans. "You said you'd fuck me, and all you're doin' is runnin' your mouth like usual. I thought we already established you're not gonna get me off like that."

She couldn't see his smile, but she felt it as his mouth rested against her temple, and her stomach flipped for no good reason at all.

"I remember exactly what it takes to get you off. I did it three times last night, or did you forget that already?"

"How could I forget when you constantly remind me?" She tugged down his fly and freed his cock from his boxer briefs, wrapping her fingers around the substantial girth. "Someone who feels the need to boast about their accolades all the time is usually compensatin' for something."

"Does it feel like I'm compensatin' for something to you?"

No... No, it absolutely did not. It felt like Cole was even bigger than she remembered, which was saying something. But of course, she wasn't going to tell him that. Wasn't going to boost his already-inflated ego any more. "I don't feel much of anything right now because you haven't made good on your promise yet."

With a growl, Cole gripped her under her ass and lifted her up, pressing her back against the pantry door with a thud that most definitely could be heard outside the kitchen. "I'm startin' to think you really do wanna be caught in here with as much as you're runnin' your mouth."

She panted at the thought, unable to stop herself from rocking her hips, desperate for friction. Desperate for *him*. "If you want me to shut up, you need to work harder than this."

"Christ, you drive me fucking *crazy*." He pinned her to the door with his hips as he reached for his wallet, the hard length of him teasing exactly where she was aching for him.

And all she could think about was what would happen if someone came into the kitchen looking for her. Would she be able to keep quiet while he thrust his length deep inside if someone called her name from the other side of the door? If Mr. Cartwright or Mrs. Waltmore came looking for her? If her sister happened to come back or if Nat popped in to talk about the pictures?

The backs of Cole's fingers brushed against her pussy through her panties as he sheathed himself, and she squirmed at the contact, desperate for more. He chuckled under his breath as he slid her panties to the side and slipped two fingers inside her.

"Did you walk around like this all day?" He pumped his fingers into her, the pressure and speed exactly what she wanted. Exactly what she needed. Exactly what she'd been waiting all day for. "With your needy little pussy drippin' 'cause of what I didn't give her today?"

Tossing her head back, she gripped his neck and bit her lip hard to stifle a moan, closing her eyes as she rocked her hips to the rhythm he'd set. Lord, why did his words throw gasoline on the fire already raging inside her? She wanted to smack him...and then climb on top of him and ride his length until she came.

"Don't you ever shut up?" she asked through panted breaths.

He pressed a kiss to her neck as he withdrew his fingers and gripped his length, using it to nudge aside her panties. "Not when I know exactly how hot it makes you. Think I could make you come with just my words?"

"You—"

But before she could finish and lie about what his words did to her, he stole her breath as he thrust inside, filling her to the brink in one swift motion. She sobbed out a moan and clutched him tighter to her, holding on for dear life as he pumped his hips relentlessly, his cock driving deep and hitting that spot inside her that'd made her see stars last night.

As he rested his forehead on her shoulder, his breaths ghosted across her chest, his fingers digging into her flesh as he worked them both toward ecstasy. "Christ, how can this be real? How can you feel so fucking good? Even better than in my dreams," he said under his breath, the words spoken almost more to himself than to her.

But they might as well have come out of her own mouth for as much as she felt them. He was right. She'd never had this kind of explosive connection with anyone she'd been with in the past. Couldn't imagine she'd ever be able to find it again in the future once Cole was long gone.

She clung to his broad shoulders, the fabric of his T-shirt bunching under her fingers as she tried desperately to hold in any whimpers or moans. Aware of just how many people were still milling about the inn who would be able to hear her.

"You're tryin' so hard to be quiet, aren't you, firecracker?" He bottomed out inside her and rotated his hips, gripping her ass tight as he worked her clit against the base of his cock. "Tryin' so hard not to let anyone know what you're doin' in here with me."

She moaned low under her breath, then bit her lip to attempt to stifle it, the thought making her pussy flutter around his length.

Cole grunted in response, his fingers digging into her flesh as his thrusts sped up. "What would someone think if they came lookin' for you and saw you ridin' my cock like this? I may have you up against this door, but there's no denyin' it's you who's fucking me, is there? Workin' that tight little pussy down on me and drivin' me out of my goddamn mind."

"*Cole.*" She sobbed his name on nothing more than a breath, her entire body tightening around him until she broke into a thousand blissful pieces, her pussy pulsing in time with his thrusts.

"That's it...*fuck.*" He settled deep inside her, his mouth open against her neck as he spilled himself inside her, his groan caught in the space between them.

She held him to her as their bodies came down from the high they'd given each other, grateful for the darkness still surrounding them. Because as sure as she was that one night with him hadn't been enough, she was even more certain now that two wouldn't do either.

CHAPTER 9

Cole didn't know what the hell he thought he was doing. He had no business taking Sadie to bed, and he had no business fucking her up against the door to the inn's pantry, and he had no business dragging her back into his room nightly.

But more than any of those, he sure as hell had no business thinking about her near constantly throughout the day and wondering things like if she enjoyed Mexican food because he was considering picking it up for dinner, and maybe he should get some for her too.

He hadn't made it more than five minutes without his thoughts circling around to her. And they weren't even acceptable thoughts, like how irritating or self-righteous she could be. Nope. Instead, he focused on how soft her skin was, how sweet she tasted, how much he loved when she pushed back and made him work for it. After sleeping with her the first time, he'd made the mistake of spending the following day in the inn's conference room. And it'd been too much—he'd known it would be, but he hadn't been able to help himself. Having that much unfettered access to her had crushed his normally rock-solid focus.

So, he'd—perhaps naïvely—assumed that if he simply went back to business as usual and spent his day in the office, the near-constant thoughts of Sadie would leave him the hell alone. Because there was no denying that he had to do something. It'd only been a few days, but if he didn't get control of the situation, his work was going to suffer, and that was unacceptable.

Well, he most definitely didn't have the situation under control. He didn't have anything under control—least of all his dick—and it pissed him off.

She'd wrecked him. Plain and simple. Though he shouldn't have been surprised. The little witch was wily like that.

He'd skipped lunch today, so he left the office a little early...absolutely not because he wanted to get back to the Starlight and to Sadie all that much sooner. Besides, his evening was already spoken for. He had some Christmas shopping to do for his mom, sister, and niece. And if Sadie happened to have suggestions for him, well, he wouldn't look a gift horse in the mouth. He wasn't a complete jack-ass, despite what she thought.

He strolled into the inn, hating how his gaze immediately shot to the front desk and where he usually found her every day after work.

Except today, she wasn't there.

In fact, the entire inn was empty and silent, something that never happened this early in the evening. He walked farther into the space and then heard voices coming from the back of the inn. Cole headed in that direction. In the direction he'd walked the other day when he'd found Sadie in the kitchen, looking like a walking wet dream and making him lose all rational thought.

Today, however, when he poked his head around the corner, it wasn't Sadie who greeted him. Well, not Sadie alone, anyway. Instead, several apron-clad people surrounded the large island in the center of the room, and Sadie stood at the head of it all, a bright smile on her face.

"Just like that, Mr. Cartwright," Sadie said to the older, balding man on her right who was using a rolling pin on some cookie dough. "I told you you'd be able to bake these."

The overwhelming scent of cinnamon hung in the air, and it transported Cole straight back to his momma's house on Christmas Eve. She loved to bake, and every year, she spent the days leading up to the holiday preparing, all so she could assemble tins for friends and neighbors. Christmas Eve was the final day in her baking marathon and reserved for her—and thus his—favorite cookies.

Next to the man, an older woman with chin-length gray hair said, "You've managed something I haven't been able to in forty years. He's always content to wait for the holiday baking to commence before he participates."

Sadie grinned at the couple. "I *have* heard the way to a man's heart is through his stomach, so I guess that's true with you. Did you win him over with cookies, Mrs. Cartwright?"

"No, she won me over with—*oof*." Mr. Cartwright rubbed his stomach where his wife had smacked him.

Mrs. Cartwright looked down her nose at her husband. "Nobody here needs to hear any of your tall tales."

Across the island, a woman in her late forties smiled. "No offense to you two, but I'd rather hear about what men the lovely Sadie has been able to snag thanks to her baking skills."

"*Ohh*, me too!" Mrs. Cartwright said, completely abandoning her slab of dough. "I like how you think, Glinda."

"Since when do you need to live vicariously through someone else?" a short, stocky man next to Glinda said.

"Since we got here, Harold, and I saw that this gorgeous woman doesn't have a ring on her finger. And that is, quite frankly, ludicrous. Are the men of Havenbrook a little slow?"

Sadie laughed, and Cole felt something pinch deep in his chest. Glinda was right—Sadie was gorgeous, and any man in his right mind would be lucky to call her his. So then, what did that make him? Because as much as he thought about Sadie, and as much as he couldn't deny their sexual chemistry, he had absolutely no intention of pursuing this any further than the bedroom. That was all he *could* do.

He wasn't a forever kind of guy anymore. He had been at one time, but he had no plans or intentions to return to that kind of life. Not when the last time ended like it did.

"Not slow so much as just the same group of men I've been around my whole life," Sadie said. "If I haven't dated them, there's a reason for that."

"Ahh," Mrs. Cartwright said with a knowing smile. "Small-town living at its finest."

Sadie offered a single-shouldered shrug. "Pretty much. Normally I love it, but it does make things challengin' in the romance department."

"Well, there must be *someone* who's snagged your interest," Glinda said, and Cole stepped closer.

He had no idea what part of him craved hearing his name from her lips right now. Especially when he had absolutely no intention of pursuing a real relationship with her, but he couldn't deny he did all the same.

"There's, um... There's..." Sadie paused, darting her gaze around the space until finally it landed on him where he stood in the doorway, eavesdropping like a creep. "Cole."

And even though he knew it wasn't in response to the question Glinda had asked, his gut still clenched over his name on her lips.

As if on cue, all the other heads in the room whipped in his direction, and he cleared his throat, offering a wave. "Hi."

"Oh! Well now... It seems she's been holding out on us," Mrs. Cartwright said under her breath, though he had no trouble hearing her from where he stood.

"What are you doin' here?" Sadie asked him. "I don't

remember seein' your name on the sign-up sheet for the class."

Right, the baking class that he'd heard murmurs about since he'd started staying there. A baking class that he'd written off, but now he sort of wished he'd had the foresight to sign up for, if only to have an excuse to be in Sadie's presence.

Cole cleared his throat and adjusted the strap of his messenger bag from where it hung on his shoulder. "I didn't. I just—" *couldn't find you and had to go and search...* "—heard voices, so I came to see what was goin' on."

"Well, you should come in," Glinda said. "There's plenty of room."

"Yes! In fact, you can take our spot. My back's acting up. I think I should go lie down," Mrs. Cartwright said, already untying her apron.

"But we haven't even baked the cookies yet," Mr. Cartwright said before his wife not so subtly jabbed an elbow into his side. She hissed something under her breath that Cole probably did not care to know about, considering the speed with which the older man removed his apron. Mr. Cartwright cleared his throat. "Yes, and I have to find ice for her back. Sorry we can't stay."

"Thanks, Sadie! We learned a lot." Mrs. Cartwright waved before pushing her husband out the door.

Glinda watched this play out before slapping a hand to her forehead. "Oh, darn it! I forgot we signed up for...that thing. In the...um...Square." She removed her apron and then did the same for her husband, who looked on with questioning eyes.

"There's nothing going on in the Square tonight," Sadie said, her brow pinched.

"No, I'm sure of it," Glinda said. "I've got my notes about it in our room. So we're just going to go get those now. You two have fun!"

Without another word, the woman dragged her husband behind her, flashing Cole a smile and a wink as she passed.

"But what about all the cookies?" Sadie asked to their retreating forms, but it was just her and Cole now, the other couples long gone.

"Is this where you tell me I sure know how to clear a room?" Cole asked, stepping into the space.

Sadie breathed out a laugh and shook her head, glancing down at the abandoned sections of dough rolled out on the island. "Well, there's no denyin' you do." She heaved out a sigh, her shoulder slumping. "Now I've gotta bake and frost all of these myself, I guess, even though I already baked mine for the day."

"Maybe I can help," he said, his mouth three steps ahead of his brain, because there was no way he would have spoken those words if he'd given himself half a second to think about it.

But instead of doing the logical thing like leaving as quickly as the other couples did and locking himself in his suite where he couldn't be tempted by this siren, he hung up his messenger bag on the hook just inside the doorway and removed his suit jacket. He turned to Sadie, unbuttoning his cuffs, then rolled up his sleeves as he walked toward her.

"*You're* gonna help?" she asked with a heavy dose of skepticism in her tone.

"You should know by now I'm a man of many talents, and I'm very good with my hands, firecracker."

Much to his smug satisfaction, Sadie's cheeks flamed, making him wonder if she was recalling the evening activities they'd shared.

"So, what're we makin'?" he asked, slipping one of the discarded aprons on and tying it at his back.

She shot him a disbelieving gaze. "I doubt you're familiar."

"Try me."

She was silent for long moments before finally relenting with a sigh. "If you'd know them as anything, it'd be by the name Cinnamon Stars. But what they're actually called is—"

"*Zimtsterne.*" Just like he'd thought. He'd recognize that scent anywhere.

She snapped her gaze up to his, surprise—and maybe delight?—on her face. "You know them?"

He grabbed the discarded rolling pin and went to work on the slab of dough that wasn't quite even. "Not only do I know them, but I've baked probably a thousand in my life."

"Seriously?"

"Yep. My mom makes them every year for Christmas. Family tradition."

Sadie was frozen for long moments before she seemed to knock herself out of it and round the island to stand on Cole's side in the spot Mrs. Cartwright vacated. "Elise and I used to make them with my grandma right here in this kitchen."

Cole hummed and made a point of glancing around at the otherwise empty room, save for them. "And yet, Elise is nowhere to be found."

Since he'd started staying at the Starlight, he'd noticed Sadie's sister had been exceptionally absent from the inn. Elise seemed to burden Sadie with the vast majority of the responsibilities, something that rubbed him the wrong way. But that wasn't so hard to understand—Cole hated when things weren't fair, and this was no exception.

Sadie shrugged and went to work on the other pieces of dough, making sure they were rolled out evenly. "She's not much of a baker. What about you? Bakin' with your mom—that's unexpected."

"Yeah, well, there are a very small handful of people in the world whom I'd do anything for, and she's one of them. So, when she says bake, I say how much."

Sadie's face softened right before Cole's eyes. "That's sweet. And not at all what I imagined when it came to you."

He raised an eyebrow. "Hard to picture me with a family?"

"Little bit. You don't exactly scream family man."

Well, that was something they could agree on, at least. And it was important to him that she knew just exactly how much of a family man he wasn't. He wouldn't mind having her warm his sheets for the foreseeable future, but he had absolutely no intention of her doing so under any illusions.

"I'm not. But it's my mom," he finished with a shrug, because that was all there was to say.

"Tell me about her. What kind of a woman raised Cole Donovan?"

He plucked one of the star-shaped cookie cutters from the bowl in the center of the island. "Comin' from you, that sounds like an insult."

Sadie huffed out a laugh and held up her hands. "No, I'm genuinely curious. Objectively speakin', you're hard-workin', tenacious, and confident."

"Otherwise known as too involved in my job, stubborn, and arrogant."

"Hey, you said it, not me."

As much as he tried to stop it, he couldn't keep his lips from tipping up in the corners even while he focused his efforts on pressing the star cookie cutters into the dough. "Everything I learned, I learned from her. She's a single mom and the strongest person I know."

Silence descended on the room for so long that Cole finally glanced in Sadie's direction, only to find her staring at him with a look he couldn't quite decipher.

He cleared his throat, ready to take the spotlight off himself. "What about you? Has it been hard on you and your sister now that your folks spend half the year in Florida?"

"It's not too bad. We stay pretty busy at the inn, plus they're happy." Sadie's brow pinched as she glanced up at him. "Wait...how'd you know that?"

"I might be new to Havenbrook, but that doesn't mean I don't know the goings-on of the townsfolk. Not much is a secret around here."

And if it was, it didn't stay that way for long. Which was something they would both do well to remember.

Cole didn't think his clients would care much about who he spent his after-hours time with, but he had no doubt hers would be horrified to find out she'd involved herself with someone whose job was the antithesis of hers.

But what Cole couldn't figure out was why he even cared.

PRIGHTON WALSH

CHAPTER 10

Every year in mid-December, the Starlight Haven Inn hosted a space for the townsfolk to gather and watch a moonlit holiday movie. In the two weeks leading up to the event, they held a vote on what that year's movie would be, and this year, *Elf* had won out, much to Sadie's delight —never mind that she wouldn't get a chance to see more than a passing glance of it.

She loved their property every day of the year, but it was something extra special during the holidays. White lights draped the gazebo, as well as the pine trees surrounding the vast backyard. Wreaths hung on each fence post, and strings of bulbed white lights surrounded the area in front of the inflatable screen where townsfolk settled in with their chairs and blankets for an evening of fun.

No matter the temperature, this night was always attended by a vast majority of residents, and Sadie did all she could to make it as comfortable for them as possible. A hot chocolate and coffee bar with various fixings was set up on the patio next to the inn for attendees to help themselves, The Willow Tree provided spirits to warm the guests in another way entirely, and strategically placed fire tables gave off some heat for the years it got a little chilly.

"You outdid yourself this year," Rory, Sadie's cousin and Nat's eldest sister, said as she walked up, two steaming cups in her hands.

Sadie smiled and gave her a hug. "You're too sweet. Are the girls here too?"

Rory lifted her chin to a spot on the lawn where her boyfriend, Nash, sat with her two daughters, the three of them laughing. "Yep, and they're desperate for me to get my butt over there because they haven't had enough sugar today."

Sadie chuckled. "Well, tell them all I said hey."

"Come tell 'em yourself. It'd do you some good to take a little break."

Sadie snorted. "You're a fine one to talk. Was it just my imagination, or did you rearrange the drink bar while you were over there?"

Rory shrugged, completely unrepentant. "Just makin' it more efficient so you could get twice as many people through the line in the same amount of time. Now, if you'll excuse me, I'm gettin' the stink eye from Ella 'cause I'm holdin' up her hot chocolate. And I meant what I said— take a break and come see us if you get a chance."

Sadie nodded in agreement, though she doubted it

would happen. It wasn't unusual for her to be running around the majority of the evening. After all, the event took place on her property, and the fine folks of Haven-brook loved to chat about nothing and everything all at once, even while classic holiday movies played in the background.

Normally, she loved it. Loved hearing about what unique gift Carol found for her group of girlfriends, and what must-have toy Sharon snagged for her grandson, but this year, it felt exceptionally irritating.

In more ways than one.

Because not only could she not focus on the merri-ment, the laughter, or the community this event had always cultivated, but what she actually *was* focusing on was the man who stood on the other side of the yard in jeans and a black wool jacket, a beanie hiding the hair Sadie loved to thrust her fingers into. The same man who'd starred in her dreams every night this week. The one who'd driven her wild with need one minute, and then surprised the hell out of her by sharing an unexpected glimpse into his life in the next.

He stood next to the Cartwrights and the Waltmores—the two couples who'd bailed on Monday's baking class—his gaze focused on the women, who seemed to be talking his ear off. But every once in a while, he'd glance in her direction, and her stomach would bottom out.

They'd fallen into a rhythm this week. One she could honestly say she'd never expected, and certainly not with him. With the exception of a couple of one-off meetings,

Cole hadn't worked from the conference room again, and she couldn't bring herself to ask him why. Had it been as distracting for him as it was for her?

Instead, he left every morning while she was in the kitchen making breakfast for the guests, and she didn't see him again until he stepped through the door that evening, his gaze immediately connecting with hers and sending shivers down her spine.

Mostly because she knew exactly what the night would hold. They'd begun sharing meals from across the gathering space in the inn—either he'd bring something back and offer her his "extras," or she'd *accidentally* make too much and offer him the same. They never technically ate together, but they might as well have for the conversations they carried out while he sat in front of the fireplace and she stood behind the front desk—both too far and not nearly far enough.

Besides the unexpected conversations, they also hadn't managed to go a single night without falling into each other's arms, or into Cole's bed. Hell, the night he'd taken her in the kitchen pantry, they'd proven a bed was inconsequential. Not exactly her best decision, but she was finding her decision-making skills had left the building when it came to Cole.

"—just the cutest little thing." Margot, a new guest who'd checked in earlier that afternoon, placed her hand on Sadie's arm and glanced around at the bustle of people, everyone still settling in to their places on the lawn. "It's like y'all live in a Hallmark movie over here. Honestly, I've never seen anything like it."

Sadie shook her head to dispel the completely inappropriate thoughts and instead focused her attention on her guest where it should have been all along.

She smiled up at the tall woman who looked intimidating at first glance, her face all sharp, harsh lines, her hair buzzed short, but whose voice and demeanor were as sweet as honey. "I'm so glad you're enjoyin' your stay so far. You really lucked out that we happened to have this on the schedule on your first night. Maybe you can talk your town into doin' something like this? I'd be happy to offer any details I can."

"Oh, no." Margot waved a hand through the chilly December air. "I don't want to have anything to do with the people in my town. Why do you think I traveled a couple hours to get away from there?" She laughed without restraint, the sound loud and infectious, and Sadie couldn't help but chuckle along.

Before she could respond, someone tugged on her right coat sleeve—just another in the line tonight who desperately needed her attention for something or other.

"I hope you have a wonderful night. Let me know if you need anything," she said before turning toward the attention-seeker.

"You know, if you started chargin' for this, you could make a pretty little penny," Edna—the attention-seeker—said, leaning so close her reindeer antlers nearly poked

Sadie in the eye. "I'd be happy to sit at the front and take tickets for you."

Sadie shook her head with a laugh. "Like I've been tellin' you every year, we're happy to do this without expectin' any payment."

"Seems to me it'd just make sense to be compensated." Edna elbowed Sadie in the side and leaned closer as if they were sharing a secret. "Especially when there's at least one other thing you'd rather be doin' tonight."

Sadie's brows pinched, but before she could ask Edna about that cryptic remark, the older woman sashayed off, her lighted necklace flashing as she went.

And that was how the rest of the event played out. She never got closer than thirty feet to Cole, but the looks he pinned her with were enough to make her hungry with need. Enough to have her wet with wanting and working through the schedule to figure out when the two of them could escape to his room again. But she had so much to do to clean up tonight, and, like usual, she'd be on her own.

She absolutely shouldn't be planning what illicit thing she'd like to do to him that night, here of all places. Not with hundreds of Havenbrook residents present to witness it. Most definitely not with her next bride—one who desperately believed in happily ever afters—in attendance. She didn't need to know what Sadie was getting up to with the man who made his living off the misery of former couples.

Not only should she not be having those inappropriate daydreams about the infuriating man, but she shouldn't *want* to be so close to him under the prying eyes of everyone in town. But she couldn't help it. Couldn't help that need from overtaking her, especially when he looked at her like he was overcome with the same.

What had started out as something purely sexual had blossomed into something else she...sort of maybe wanted to explore?

And that, above all else, scared the hell out of her.

AFTER THE LAST Havenbrook resident had left and each of the Starlight's guests were tucked into their rooms for the evening, it was nearing midnight, and Sadie was exhausted. She always was after this event, but that never tamped down her desire to host it year after year. She loved seeing the happiness on the faces of her fellow residents, but more than that, she loved knowing she was the cause of it.

What she could use right now was a soak in the honeymoon suite's tub, followed by a full body massage. Either that or an orgasm. Unfortunately, her plans tonight contained neither.

She glanced toward the hallway leading to where she could get all three and had to force herself to keep walking. As much as she wanted to go knock on Cole's door and drag him across the hall to climb into that bath together, she couldn't do that. For one thing, she still had too much to do before she could think about checking out for the night. And for another, that was far too intimate for the two of them.

Wasn't it?

They'd never defined what this was between them, but Sadie could read between the lines. They were enemies turned frenemies turned fuck buddies, and she was completely fine with that. Of course she wanted the happy ending...*eventually*...but that didn't mean she couldn't enjoy a little fun on her way to it.

With a sigh, she continued to the French doors off the dining room and stepped out into the brisk night. Now that the yard was empty and the fires had all been put out, it was freezing out here. Unfortunately, she still had probably two hours of—

She startled then froze in her tracks as her gaze connected with a man at the hot chocolate and coffee station. Holding a black trash bag, Cole glanced over at her, raised an eyebrow, and then focused back on his task of clearing the long table of any garbage.

The sight stole her words for half a second before she forced herself to move. A quick glance around showed that while she'd been making sure the guests were settled in and all the residents had vacated the premises, he'd already been busy, gathering up stray blankets people had left behind and putting them in the bin Sadie had marked as Lost and Found, as well as deflating the screen, and now, apparently, garbage cleanup.

"What're you doin' out here?" she asked, stepping up to the other side of the table and matching his efforts.

He shrugged, tossing the discarded, half-drunk cups into the bag. "I saw Elise leave an hour ago, so I figured you'd be back here by yourself."

Her brow pinched, and she regarded him...this man so different from the one she'd built off nothing but her assumptions. "And that made you want to help? Doesn't sound like you..."

He huffed out a semblance of a laugh and lifted his gaze to hers. "Believe it or not, I'm not an asshole all the time."

"You're not?" she teased, reaching over and dropping some trash into the bag, their fingers brushing as she did so and sending a shock wave straight up to her shoulder.

"I said not *all* the time. But definitely a solid sixty percent."

She smiled, ignoring the way his gaze dropped to her lips, and glanced around at the space she was usually on her own to clean up. "Well, I appreciate that I benefited from the forty percent tonight."

"Well, with sixty-forty odds, it was inevitable it'd happen sooner or later."

"Cole." She reached over and gripped his forearm, squeezing until he lifted his eyes to hers. "I mean it. We tease each other a lot, but I really am grateful. This usually takes me two hours, and instead, tonight, it's going to take us ten minutes."

He hummed and tied up the bag they'd finished filling before walking over to the bins and tossing it inside. "Well, don't think too highly of me just yet."

"Why not?"

He walked toward her, not stopping until he was close enough that she could feel his breath sweeping across her lips. "Maybe I have ulterior motives."

The way he said it, low and deep and teasing, made her stomach flip like a gymnast. Had her knees going weak over thoughts of what he meant. Had her mind churning a thousand miles an hour over fantasies of what those motives might be.

She swallowed and gathered the thermal hot chocolate carafe to her chest. "And what would those be?"

After gathering the two coffee carafes in his arms, he tipped his head toward the house, and with a nod, she led the way, overly aware of how close he was. Her body was humming, like it always seemed to do in his presence, and she needed to get ahold of herself. Just because they'd spent the past few nights in each other's company didn't mean he had any plans of ravishing her again tonight.

"I seem to recall you tellin' me there's a claw-foot tub in the honeymoon suite. And I thought you could use a soak to warm up after spendin' hours outside tonight."

She snapped her gaze to his, her mind not quite able to keep up with what he was saying or the fact that it somehow echoed exactly what she'd been hoping for earlier. "You...want me to take a bath?"

He set the carafes on the counter in the kitchen, then took hers from her arms and did the same. With his hands braced on the counter on either side of her hips, he leaned toward her, invading her space and making her ache for

him even more. "No, firecracker. I want *us* to take a bath...
after I fuck you in it."

All the breath in her lungs left her in a whoosh, and
she curled her fingers over the edge of the countertop just
so she didn't dissolve into a puddle at his feet. Who *was*
this guy? Because he sure as hell wasn't the Cole Donovan
she'd conceived in her mind—the guy who aided in the
stealing of family antiques, doll collections, and ex-wives'
breasts.

But she didn't want to think about that. Couldn't bring
herself to. She just wanted to lose herself in him again—in
his arms and his words and his penetrating gaze and the
way he'd come to know her body better than anyone ever
had before.

Because if she took time to actually think about it, to
dissect what this meant—or worse, what he meant to her—
she'd have to come up with some answers. And the truth
was...she didn't have any.

CHAPTER 11

Cole never should have slept with Sadie. Not because it hadn't been amazing, and not because it wasn't the best sex of his life, but rather because now he couldn't seem to go more than an hour without thinking about her and recalling exactly what it felt like to be surrounded by all that heaven. Hadn't been able to go a day without seeking her out. Without settling himself between those thighs and sinking deep.

Of course, it didn't help that they were practically living together, considering his temporary home was the inn where she was constantly. As soon as he stepped foot through the front door, his gaze was drawn to her like a magnet. The only thing that gave him a bit of solace was that her eyes inevitably sought him as well. And the time between when he arrived at the end of a long day and when she was able to break away from the front desk was like the longest foreplay session ever. He'd taken to camping out in the main room and working on client files there. At least, when he wasn't busy eye-fucking her as he'd been known to do.

Each encounter they had was better than the last, though he didn't know how that was possible. He also didn't know how it was possible that she'd managed to break through every wall he'd erected for himself after his divorce. She'd torn them down with her wit and her sharp tongue, and he hadn't even known what hit him. Worse, it'd been less than two weeks since the photo shoot that had started him on the path to madness.

He used to spend his days and nights working. Getting what his clients needed was his life. What he'd dedicated himself to. In recent months, it had begun to feel empty, but since Sadie, it was something else entirely. Not only had he been brainstorming ways he could negotiate to get her family antiques back from his former client—something he'd never before even considered—but he counted down the minutes until he could leave at the end of the day just to see her.

He was contemplating whether he could justify sneaking out early if he planned to sit in the main area of the inn and do some more work, when his phone rang, the call patched through from his office manager. Without an announcement of who it was, that meant it was either his sister or his mom, neither of whom called him often at work.

"Hello?"

"Oh good, honey. I'm so glad I caught you."

Cole leaned back in his chair and swiveled from side to side, welcoming this distraction. "Hey, Momma. Everything okay?"

Charlotte Donovan might be a fully grown woman who could take care of herself—she'd proven that as she'd raised two kids on her own—but he couldn't help himself from asking, especially when she didn't usually call the office.

She tutted on the other line, and the smile in her voice rang through when she said, "You're sweet. I'm just fine. But..."

The long pause had his hackles rising, and he sat up in his seat, bracing his forearms on the desk. "What's wrong? Is it Carly? Whitney?"

"No, no...your sister and niece are just fine. I didn't mean to worry you."

"Well, hell, Momma. Just tell me what you need to say before you give me a heart attack."

She blew out a long sigh. "It's Maryann's girl, Jemma. You remember her? She's a few years older than you."

Considering his hometown was as small as Havenbrook, yeah, he knew her. Just like he knew pretty much every other resident there. Knew her bully of a husband too.

"Yeah, I remember. What's goin' on?"

"She's been... Well, she's been havin' some troubles with her husband, Darryl."

His gut tightened over how his momma said the words —careful and slow like molasses—and he grabbed a pen and the legal pad he kept on his desk, ready to jot down any notes. "All these pauses are killin' me, Momma. Just come out and say it. What kind of troubles?"

"She finally pressed charges against him."

Cole blew out a breath and tightened his grip on the pen as memories of the too-close-for-comfort brush his sister had had with just such an asshole bombarded him. "What does she need?" he asked without hesitation.

"I know you're busy up there, and I know you only do divorces now, but—"

"Momma," he said sternly. "What does she need?"

She paused only a moment more before she said, "A lawyer, and she can't afford to pay for one."

Not the first time he'd been approached with a plea for pro bono help, but the first time he'd known immediately he'd take the case. "Does she know you're callin' me?"

"Yes, but she's not real happy about it. She's proud. You know how it is. Doesn't want to take a handout."

Yeah, he knew firsthand how that was, having grown up with a single mom, working two jobs and refusing to let him drop out of high school to help her pay the bills. "I'll figure something out to smooth it over with her. What's her number?"

After rattling it off, she sighed and said, "You've got such a big heart, Cole."

He used to, back before his life had been turned inside out. But somewhere along the way, he'd detached himself. For so long, he'd prided himself on being heartless. That was what he needed to be after he'd found his wife—the woman he'd been with nearly half his life—in bed with his best friend. And in the months and years following their betrayal, he'd found it was easier that way. Easier to work for guys like Travis and Alec, who were nothing more than pigs disguised as men and who always seemed to find him as sure as the sun rising each morning. Easier to demand their unnecessary requests fueled solely on contempt than it was to actually care. Sure, there were the anomalies who found their way to him—like Rory Haven just last year— but by and large, he served self-serving assholes.

And he was tired of it. So fucking tired of it. He'd been feeling this way for months. But now that he had someone as bright and good as Sadie in his life—or at least, in his bed —it made him want to do better. To be better.

And this was exactly where he could start.

CHAPTER 12

S adie had no idea why the heavens had shone down upon her today, but it was clear she'd done something good. Or, more likely, Elise felt guilty for continually bailing on her, and that was why she'd shoved Sadie out the door that evening, saying she had everything under control.

Sadie had been reluctant to leave, of course. Sip and Shop was a huge event in Havenbrook and for the businesses participating—Starlight included—but it would be mostly foot traffic for the inn tonight. The real business would come tomorrow and in the days and weeks following, when people called to book staycations or mini getaways thanks to their enticements tonight. Enticements like her lemon poppy seed and blueberry crumble muffins. But since she hadn't been able to attend this the past three years—too busy trying to get their bearings at the inn—it hadn't taken a lot of coaxing on Elise's part to get Sadie to say yes.

She strolled down the packed streets of Havenbrook, busier than usual. Or maybe Sadie had just forgotten what typical was. Willow had done such a fantastic job decorating the Square, and Sadie had little doubt her cousin had spent weeks ironing out the details. Lampposts lining the streets were strung with alternating white and red lights, their metal adorned with garland. Storefronts around the Square continued the theme, their archways and doors laden with twinkling lights, red bows, and enough mistletoe that anyone could get into trouble.

What would Cole do if he were here? If they were strolling these streets together and they happened under a sprig of mistletoe? Would he kiss her when it wouldn't lead straight to a bed? When there were people around... witnesses to their affection? It'd been less than two weeks since their first kiss, but Sadie was wrapped up in this whirlwind as much as—more than—she'd been with her last long-term boyfriend of two years. Was she really that hard up for affection, or was there truly something there between her and Cole?

It felt like there was. During the sex, obviously, but after, too. When they lay, tangled in the sheets and each other's bodies, their breaths as uneven as her heart. It was during their whispered conversations about absolutely nothing of consequence that she wondered if there might be something more there between them.

Tucking her hands in the pockets of her navy pea coat,

she inhaled deeply and closed her eyes, loving that just the scents of the season were enough to make her feel at home. She'd never understood why her parents fled even farther south in the winter months. But as soon as they'd retired, they bolted to Fort Myers, Florida, each year with little more than a backward glance. They'd breathed a collective sigh of relief when they'd found out Nana Rollins had left the inn to Sadie and Elise.

"So, you *did* look at them."

Sadie startled at the voice in her ear and spun around to find Nat's smiling face. "Hey! I didn't know you were comin' back to town so soon."

"Asher talked me into it since I was still stateside and he was plannin' a trip home. The things I do for that guy..." she grumbled, shaking her head as she narrowed her eyes at the Square and the happy, festive townsfolk, the Grinch come to life.

Sadie snorted. "And to see your family?"

Nat waved a hand through the air. "Yeah, yeah, that too."

"When does Asher get in?"

"Tonight." She pulled out her phone and glanced at the screen. "He already landed, actually, so he should be here anytime."

"And you think he's gonna be able to find you in all this?" Sadie asked, gesturing to the throngs of people lining the streets, their laughter and voices ringing into the night.

Nat wiggled her phone in front of Sadie. "That's why we've got these neat little things." She fell into step beside

125

Sadie, bumping their shoulders together. "Speaking of, can I assume your fancy communication device suffered a premature death, and that's why I haven't heard back about those completely amazing and utterly hot pictures I sent a week ago?"

"What completely amazing and utterly hot pictures?" a deep male voice asked.

Nat spun around, squealing as she threw her arms around Asher, one of her two oldest and best friends. He returned the embrace, tucking his face into her neck and squeezing her tight to him. Sadie knew they were just friends. Which meant she was completely aware it was just her line of work that had her starry-eyed as she watched them reunite, the joy on their faces at seeing each other lighting something hopeful inside her.

If Cole ever looked at her like that, she might believe they actually had something more than just sex.

After several moments, they pulled apart, and Asher slung his arm around Nat, shooting Sadie a grin. "Hey, Sadie. How've you been?"

"I'm—"

"She's bein' an idiot."

Sadie huffed. "Excuse you."

"Well, you are. I mean, *look* at these!" Nat held up her phone for Asher to see. "Remember how Anne and her husband came down with the flu, and I thought I was gonna be completely fucked for that magazine spread?"

Asher's eyebrows lifted. "Yeah. How'd you figure your way out of that one?"

"She suckered *me* into doin' it," Sadie said.

Asher glanced over at her and flashed her a smile. "Bet she didn't even have to sell her soul, did she? This girl could talk a chair into givin' her its legs."

Nat shrugged. "I'm not even sorry. How can I be when *this* is the outcome?" She held the phone up a mere inch away from Asher's face.

He leaned back and plucked the phone out of her grasp, before glancing down, his eyebrows inching up his forehead. He whistled low and cupped a hand around his neck. "Damn," he said with conviction, swiping his thumb over the screen to view the remaining images.

"I know, right? Who knew strangers could have this much chemistry?"

"I told you we weren't strangers, remember? He was Alec's divorce attorney."

Nat wrinkled her nose. "Wait...the asshole who got him all of y'all's antiques?"

Why did Sadie's stomach clench at that descriptor? It'd been the same that she'd used for years, but somehow, now, it felt troublesome. She swallowed down the uneasy feeling and tucked her hair behind her ear. "The very one."

But maybe this was exactly what Sadie needed at this point. A reminder as to why she couldn't pursue anything with Cole—he had no interest in the happy ending, and that was Sadie's endgame. Certainly, the only thing she'd be willing to put effort into while she struggled with the inn.

"That just doesn't make any sense," Nat said, shaking

her head. "When I showed Rory these pictures, she said he was *her* divorce attorney. And Rory wouldn't put up with a complete asshole."

Asher laughed. "Actually, I'm pretty sure she'd enjoy an asshole, just so she could put him in his place."

"He's not wrong, and Rory was more interested in findin' Nash after she'd seen these than she was in talkin' any shit about Cole."

Sadie's face flamed at Nat's insinuation even as she rolled her eyes. "Now you're just bein' a brat about it."

Nat held up her hand and laughed. "Swear! Well, I mean, after she got over the fact that the guy in those pictures was her same hard-ass attorney. She said he's a good guy, if a little aloof. And he got her everything she wanted in the divorce."

Sadie's brow furrowed. "But didn't Rory's ex get the house?"

Nat shrugged. "She didn't want it. Cole thought she was crazy for givin' it up, but she wanted to make it on her own. So instead, he got her half the house's value in IRAs or whatever for the girls' college funds." She turned to Sadie with glee in her eyes. "And he *completely* decimated Sean in court, which was, apparently, a delight to watch, according to my sister."

Dammit. This *wasn't* what she needed. Not if she was intent on keeping Cole in the fuck buddy category—a category she'd never, in her entire life, used.

"That doesn't prove he's a good guy," Sadie said,

though her voice was weak. "That proves he gets exactly what his clients want."

Case in point, the lying cheater holding their family's antiques hostage for the simple reasoning that Elise hadn't been willing to overlook his indiscretions.

"Wait a minute," Asher said, snapping his fingers. "Is that...Donovan or something? Guy moved here a couple years ago?"

"Yeah, Cole." Nat nodded.

"My sister just told me about him. Called me last night so damn excited. I thought it was about me comin' to town today, but nope. She's good about keepin' me humble. Apparently, he contacted the shelter yesterday and offered his services for any domestic abuse cases. Pro bono."

"No shit?" Nat asked, brows raised. "It doesn't surprise me, considerin' the tough spot he helped me out of. I fucked up his whole week, but he shuffled it around just so he could do the pics with Sadie. And thank God for that, because without him, I wouldn't have these." Nat wiggled her phone again, shoving it in Sadie's face for good measure.

"Yeah, yeah," Sadie said. "I get it. The pics are great. Very...hot."

Nat snorted. "That's an understatement. I'm actually glad to know the inn didn't burn down."

"What?" Sadie snapped her attention to her cousin, panic gripping her. "Why would you say that? Why would the inn burn down?"

Nat rolled her eyes and linked her arms through both

Sadie's and Asher's, guiding them farther along their path. "Relax. I didn't mean literally. I just thought, what with the combustible chemistry between you two, that you'd light it on fire the second you walked inside."

Sadie exhaled a relieved breath but otherwise schooled her expression. Except she'd never quite learned how to stop a blush in its tracks. Combustible chemistry was *also* an understatement. They did burn for each other when-ever they were in the same vicinity. She'd left her post at the inn earlier and earlier each night, just so she could get to Cole faster. But could anyone blame her, when he sat in the common area, his shirt sleeves rolled up, tie loosened, and hair amiss? She felt his eyes on her so often, she was surprised he even managed to get work done. And when she closed down the computer for the day, he didn't take them off her as he packed up his things and summoned her to his room with little more than a quirk of his eyebrow and a head tilt.

And then... Oh, then, the real fun began.

Her face flamed, and with the number of lights illumi-nating the Square, there was absolutely no hope of hiding it from Nat.

Her cousin gasped and yanked her arm out of Sadie's, pointing an accusatory finger at her. "I knew it! I *knew* something was happenin' between y'all. There's no fucking way two people can have that kind of intense chemistry and not be fucking."

"My best friend, always so tactful and timid," Asher said dryly.

Sadie's gaze shot around to the passersby, worried who'd overheard her cousin's declaration. Fortunately, the Havenbrook residents weren't paying them any attention, for once in her life, and she'd never been more grateful.

"Would you keep your voice down?" Sadie hissed. "Hell, Natalie. If I wanted the entire town to know, I would've told Edna."

Nat clapped a hand over her mouth, her eyes sparkling above it.

Sadie huffed out a breath and shook her head. "I don't know what you're so excited about. Whatever was happenin' between me and Cole, we worked it out of our systems," she said, absolutely lying through her teeth. She had no idea how Cole felt, but she was nowhere near getting him out of her system.

"Why?" Nat asked, eyes wide. "Is he not good in bed? Tiny dick?" She shook her head in disappointment. "It's always the hot, confident ones, you know? You think they're workin' with a lot, and...not so much."

"Please," Asher said, his tone flat, "tell me more about all the penises you think about."

Nat rolled her eyes and blindly reached back until she connected with Asher's face and then shoved lightly. "Don't pretend like this is new information for you."

"It wasn't either of those things," Sadie admitted.

When she offered nothing further, Nat said, "Okay, and *why* isn't this continuing? Look, don't get me wrong— I'm glad he fucked some life back into your vagina after the long dry spell you told me about."

Sadie cupped her hand over her eyes and shook her head. "Oh my *word*, Nat. Why do I tell you these things?"

"Honestly, I'm not sure. But back to the matter at hand. Why aren't you poppin' a quarter in and takin' that pony for another ride?"

Sadie really wished she'd made a point to stop by The Willow Tree—the town's one and only bar—immediately upon her arrival downtown to indulge in this year's holiday drink. Then maybe she'd be tipsy enough to have this conversation. "Did you seriously just tell me to ride him like a pony?"

Nat stifled a laugh but sobered at Sadie's expression and held up a hand in surrender. "Okay, I'll be serious. Promise." Nat crossed her finger over her heart. "Is it because of Elise and what Cole got for Alec?"

"Partially..."

Asher cupped a large hand on the back of Nat's neck at the same time she pursed her lips to the side, as if holding herself back from saying something. What would it be like to have that kind of connection with someone? Who knew you so well, inside and out, that they could anticipate what you were going to do before you did it?

Finally, Nat said, "Okay, you said partly, so what else is holdin' you back? Because it's clearly not the sex. Right? You said he could get down..."

"No, I didn't, but you keep tryin' to pull that out of me."

Natalie tossed her head back and groaned. "I'm just so invested in this. I mean, would this even have happened if

I hadn't talked you into these pictures?" Nat gasped and gripped Sadie's forearm. "If you guys end up gettin' married, I call maid of honor! I know your twin should technically have dibs on that, but... No, it should for sure be me."

Sadie breathed out a laugh and sidestepped an oncoming family, her gaze lingering only briefly. "That's the thing. There won't be a wedding, because Cole is not at all interested in that."

"How do you know? Have y'all even been on an actual date?"

Not unless she counted endless orgasms and a grand total of actual days spent in bed together...

"We don't have to be for me to know that. Nat, he's lived here for more than three years, and in that time, I've never seen him date anyone. Besides that, don't you think our careers say it all?"

Nat's brow furrowed. "Lawyer and innkeeper?" she asked, confusion heavy in her tone.

"I think she probably means wedding planner and divorce attorney," Asher said, his arm slung around Nat's shoulders in an easy embrace as they walked.

"Bingo."

Nat waved a hand through the air. "Oh, who cares about all that. You plan weddings, and he plans divorces. Big fucking deal. What's the harm in givin' him a chance?"

The harm was that in all the times Sadie had imagined her Prince Charming, she might have imagined Cole's dirty-blond hair or his pale-blue eyes or his tall, hard body and how it fit so perfectly against hers. How, in only a short time, he somehow knew how she took her hot chocolate and brought her a fresh cup when he arrived at the inn, or that he could tell when she hadn't eaten supper and offered some of his pizza that just so happened to be topped with all her favorites.

But one thing she'd never imagined was falling in love with someone who believed so surely in love's inevitable demise, he'd made a career out of it.

CHAPTER 13

This was Cole's third Christmas in Havenbrook but his first time experiencing the town's famous Sip and Shop event. The streets were bustling, the Square packed with townsfolk and those who traveled in just for it. Which was exactly why he usually opted out of attending. He'd grown used to flying under the radar—when the rumors surrounding his and his ex-wife's split began surfacing, he'd made it a point to keep his private life private—but when his sister had called and told him she and her daughter were visiting him specifically to attend, he'd reluctantly agreed.

Though they both knew the reluctant part was all an act. Between her, their mom, and his niece, he could be talked into just about anything. It wouldn't surprise him if he were actually physically unable to say no to the three most important women in his life. Case in point, the call from his momma yesterday. Though he couldn't say he regretted it. After they'd hung up, he'd contacted the shelter in town, that serviced the surrounding area as well, and offered his services anytime they needed them. He'd done it so he could tell Jemma that it was something he offered to everyone, not just her. But he couldn't deny that as he'd left the office last night, he'd felt better than he had in a long time.

"I can't get over how adorable Havenbrook is," Carly said, her eyes bright as she glanced around the Square. "Seriously, I wouldn't be surprised if there was a Hallmark movie being filmed down the street."

It was late, the sky dark, but the streets were brightly lit with holiday lights. Stores were open later tonight to accommodate what appeared to be the entire population of Havenbrook, some even setting up stands outside with holiday confections and festive hot beverages to counteract the chill. Townsfolk wrapped up tightly in their winter gear strolled, arm in arm, through the streets, their laughter ringing along with the distant harmony of carolers.

Cole rolled his eyes and glanced down at his sister. "You still watch those things?"

She scoffed and lightly slapped his arm. "Of course I do. What kind of question is that? I like to be happy during the holidays, and sappy, romantic movies make me happy. I've gotten Whitney hooked on them too."

He groaned. "C'mon, Carly. Don't fill her head with idealistic garbage."

She turned to him, her eyebrows raised. "Oh, so romance is idealistic garbage?"

"That's not what I said." Though, yes, that too. Cole's life—hell, Carly's too—was proof enough of that. "What's idealistic is the idea of two people bein' together forever."

"I see someone peed in your Cheerios this mornin'."

Cole ran a hand over his jaw and shook his head. "Nothing new there."

Carly glanced ahead to Whitney, the teen's phone illuminating her face as she managed to type and walk at the same time, instinctively dodging both people and inanimate objects. Lowering her voice, she said, "Look, I know Amber totally screwed up your outlook—"

He snorted. Yeah, his ex-wife—and ex-best friend—had messed with him, but it didn't start there. "My outlook was tainted well before that. Or have you forgotten about our father? Or how about hers?" he asked, lifting a chin toward Whitney.

Their dad hadn't stuck around past Carly's first birthday, and Whitney's hadn't lasted past the positive pregnancy test. And the person he thought he'd spend the rest of his life with had turned into a cheater, so no, he didn't have a lot of positive experiences surrounding love and all the shit that came with it.

Carly exhaled a long-suffering sigh, the sound so familiar, it nearly brought a smile to his lips. He wasn't doing his job correctly as big brother if he didn't frustrate her daily. "I'm not disagreein' that those men were complete assholes. Are you sayin' that's what you are?"

"Now you're just twistin' my words."

His sister hooked her arm through Cole's, giving it a

short tug. "I just don't want you to be alone forever. Amber wasn't right for you. I could've told you that before you got married—tried to, I'm pretty sure. But that doesn't mean no one ever will be. You're only thirty-five—"

"I'm thirty-three," he grumbled.

"Whatever." She waved a hand through the air. "When you tipped over thirty, I stopped keepin' track. What I'm sayin' is, you're still young. I don't think it's healthy to lock yourself up in your house and never come out."

"I'm out this week. I'm out right now." He gestured around them to the bustling Square and all the townsfolk milling about. "I've been out for the past nearly three weeks. I don't even live—or sleep—in my home right now."

"That's different. It's not for the fun reason."

Flashes of his nights with Sadie over the past week sparked in his mind before he shut them down as fast as they'd popped up. Not because he didn't want to remember them and catalog every inch of her beautiful body, arched and begging for more of him, but because he enjoyed it too much when he did. And he refused to have that kind of reaction in front of his sister.

"Whoa, whoa, whoa," Carly asked, tugging on his jacket sleeve. "What's that look for?"

"What look?"

"Don't play dumb. That look that just came over your face. What were you thinkin' about?"

Well, he certainly couldn't tell her he'd been imagining

what it'd felt like to sink into Sadie for the first time. Or the second. Or the tenth. That'd be awkward.

"I'm not... It's not—" He was so focused on his sister and trying to figure out a way around this that he'd stopped watching where he was going, his shoulder bumping into a soft body. Cole turned toward the person, hand outstretched. "Sorry. 'scuse me."

"No prob— Oh, Cole," Sadie said, her voice ringing with surprise. She darted her gaze from him to his sister, where her arm was locked around his, and back to his face, her expression falling for a split second before the disappointment was wiped clean, complete indifference replacing it. Or maybe he'd imagined it entirely.

"Sadie. Hi."

After a few moments of silence, Carly cleared her throat. "Sadie, is it? I'm his sister, Carly. And the antisocial one with the phone permanently attached to her hands is my daughter, Whitney."

Sadie offered Carly a genuine smile, one Cole realized she'd actually bestowed upon him this week after she'd withheld it from him for years. "It's nice to meet you."

"You too. So, how do you know my brother? I wasn't aware he had any friends."

Sadie breathed out a laugh, her gaze flitting to his before landing back on Carly, expression uneasy. And though they weren't a couple—weren't even really friends —he'd had years of learning to read her body language from afar, and it was clear she didn't know how to answer. He couldn't blame her. They'd been sleeping with each other, yes, and had hours upon hours of intimate conversations in the dark of the night, but what did that make them? He had no answer for that and didn't want to come up with one.

"Don't you need to head home?" He didn't bother to layer an ounce of subtlety into his statement because his meddling sister didn't deserve it.

She huffed and rolled her eyes but tugged him down to press a kiss to his cheek. "Fine." Then, for his ears only, she said, "But don't think I'm not noticin' this ridiculous tension between y'all. And don't think we won't talk about that."

"Can't wait," he said under his breath.

With a grin, she turned toward her daughter. "Whitney, come say goodbye to Uncle Cole. It's time for us to leave."

"Oh no," Sadie said, shaking her head. "You don't have to do that. I don't want to interrupt y'all's time."

Carly waved off her concern. "No, believe me, I've had my fill of brotherly interaction today. But it was so nice to meet you," she said, authenticity ringing in her tone. "I hope I'll see you again real soon."

After receiving a hug from Carly and Whitney and a promise to text him when they arrived back home, Cole tucked his hands into his coat pockets and forced himself not to react that Sadie hadn't bolted the moment they were alone. She wore jeans tonight, the fabric nearly painted on and tucked into those knee-high boots that had dug into his ass the first time they'd slept together. Her navy pea coat was unbuttoned, revealing a bright-red fitted sweater that clung to the curves he knew the exact size and shape of. Curves he'd run his hands and mouth over every night this week. Curves he'd gripped while he'd been buried deep inside her, desperate to never leave.

He cleared his throat and shifted, willing his hard-on to subside. "I figured you'd be at the inn tonight."

"Me too, actually. But Elise must be feelin' extra guilty 'cause she practically shoved me out the door."

"That's nice of her." Though, from what he'd seen while staying there, not nearly enough to account for all that she piled on Sadie. "It's just you two at the inn?"

"Yeah. Our grandma left it to us, so we're makin' a go of it. Or tryin' to." She glanced up at him as they fell into step next to each other. "What about you? Any other siblings?"

"Nope, just Carly."

Sadie hummed, glancing toward the carolers as they strolled by, before meeting his eyes, hers twinkling with that playful gleam he'd come to recognize. "I have to admit, I was surprised to learn you weren't spawned in a hellscape somewhere and sent here strictly to make my life difficult."

"That would seem plausible, wouldn't it?"

"Overwhelmingly so."

His lips tipped up at the corners. Christ, he loved when they volleyed back and forth like this, even if it was at his expense. "Sorry to pop your theory bubble, but I was born at St. John's hospital in Forest Falls. My sister still lives in our hometown, right next door to my momma."

"Wow. That's..."

"Claustrophobic?"

She laughed, and he ignored the way the sound—once so unfamiliar in his presence—warmed his chest. What the hell was she doing to him? "No, I was gonna say sweet. With my parents all the way in Florida right now, maybe I'm just feelin' lonesome for them. It's too close for comfort for you?"

He lifted a single shoulder, keeping his eyes on their path instead of on her like he was tempted to. Always so damn tempted. "That, and I didn't want to see my ex-wife every time I went out for a run or met a client or grocery shopped."

"Ah... Small-town livin' at its finest."

When she didn't say anything else, he asked, "That's it?"

"What do you mean?"

"No crack about how you can't believe someone would actually marry me?"

She bit her lip, her gaze cataloging his face, something secretive passing behind her eyes. Finally, she hummed and shrugged. "Maybe later."

The laugh burst from him so sharply and unexpectedly, it surprised them both. Sadie startled before turning wide eyes on him, her mouth parted. He shouldn't have been held responsible for how his gaze dropped to it, remembering what it felt like to suck her lower lip just to hear her response. How he'd breathed in her moans and memorized her taste. How, no matter when he'd had her, he always seemed to crave more.

"I've never heard you laugh before," she said quietly. And then, as if she'd revealed too much, she cleared her throat and averted her gaze to the Square, lit up and still bustling now, even long after night had fallen. "It's been so long since I've been able to attend this, I almost forgot how beautiful it all is."

"It is," Cole said, never taking his eyes from her. Fuck, she took his breath away, and he knew more than anyone that he was in danger of suffocating. What the hell was he doing, mooning over this woman who craved a happy ending so much she'd made a career out of it?

He averted his gaze, focusing it on safer things. Things that didn't make him lose his mind. Things that didn't leave him aching even after they were gone. "Makes my sister jealous anyway. She swears the Square belongs in a Hallmark movie."

Sadie gasped and turned to face him, placing her hand on his arm. "She's right! It looks exactly like the downtown from the one I watched the other night."

Of course the small-town wedding planner would be invested in that shit. "Don't tell me—you're a sucker for those too."

She rolled her eyes. "Don't tell me—Mr. Divorce Attorney thinks it's all garbage. There's still probably a line of kids waitin' to sit on Santa's lap if you wanna crush any more hopes and dreams tonight."

He breathed out a laugh—when did he stop finding her

infuriating and start finding her amusing? "I'll save the kids for later. As for the romantic movies, I hate to be the bearer of bad news, but I've witnessed too much not to be jaded."

Sadie pursed her lips before nodding. "Fair enough. But I've witnessed too much not to be hopeful."

"And what about when that hopeful couple comes knockin' on my door in a year or two or ten?"

Sadie lifted a shoulder. "Then they do, but maybe that was just their path. Just because that marriage dissolved doesn't mean those two people can't still find their happy ending with others. I'd rather be hopeful that'll happen than so cynical that I don't even consider the possibility."

He *was* cynical. His life—both personal and professional—had hardened him to be, but he was thankful she wasn't jaded like him. Hopeful looked good on her.

"Sadie!" Edna called, waving as best she could while carrying two to-go cups with lids. "Been lookin' all over for you." She dressed the part of Santa's more festive grandmother, wearing flashing reindeer antlers, red and gold garland draped around her neck like a scarf, and a red velour jogging suit. "And Cole! Well... Apparently, Sadie's cookies really did the trick," she said with a not at all discreet eyebrow waggle.

"Oh no," Sadie cut in with a shake of her head. "We're not—"

"Never mind that," Edna said, though Cole wanted desperately to hear the rest of that sentence. They weren't...what? A couple? Anything more than fuck buddies? A possibility in even the vastest reach of the imagination? "I'm just glad I found you. These are yours." With a grin, she held out the cups toward him and Sadie.

"But I didn't—"

"Oh, hush now, sugar. I know you didn't, but Finn pawned them off on me, and I figured I'd pass on the bounty."

Sadie eyed the cups skeptically. "What's in 'em?"

"Peppermint hot chocolate—spiked, of course. Go on, take 'em. You look like you could use some loosenin' up. Besides, you'd be savin' me from myself. I had an...incident the last time I drank peppermint schnapps."

Having advised Edna more than once on her extracurricular activities and thus knowing exactly what kind of mischief she got into when she was completely sober, Cole didn't doubt her statement for a second.

"I'll take 'em," he offered, plucking the cups from her hands.

"Well, aren't you a gentleman," Edna cooed.

Cole brought one of the cups to his mouth, took a sip, and promptly coughed, the excessive amount of peppermint schnapps overwhelming his senses. Through choked breaths, he managed, "Finn made this?"

He'd been into The Willow Tree enough times to know Finn—one-third of the bar's owners and an accomplished bartender—knew how to make a drink. Obviously. But this...this tasted like a monkey got ahold of the liquor cabinet and dumped the entire contents into this tiny sixteen-ounce cup.

"Well...he made the base, but then I added a little

something." Edna pulled out a bedazzled flask from her coat pocket and shot them a grin. "Never can have too much. If you're not gettin' tipsy off one drink, you're doin' something wrong, kids. Now, don't do anything I wouldn't do. Which, for the record, leaves your night pretty much completely open." She waggled her eyebrows before shuffling off without a backward glance, no doubt intent to cause chaos elsewhere.

Cole sipped once again, grimacing at the strong flavor but powering through.

"You're still gonna drink that?" Sadie asked, her tone incredulous.

He glanced down at her, her cheeks pink from the cold. Reminding him of last night when she'd been flushed just like that...when he'd had his face between her legs and he'd licked up all the sweetness she had to offer before sinking inside her and making them both lose their minds. Maybe drinking in her presence wasn't his best idea, because God knew he already lacked self-control where she was concerned. "Don't want 'em to go to waste."

"But you're makin' a face every time you drink it. I didn't realize you antagonized yourself as much as you do me."

"If that were true, I'd have tricked you into drinkin' the other one."

Sadie stopped in the middle of the sidewalk and narrowed her eyes at him. "Or, you're pretendin' it's awful when it's really delicious just so you can have both." She grabbed the other cup out of his grasp. "Nice try."

Before he could stop her, she lifted it to her mouth and took a drink. She sputtered and coughed, gasping as her eyes watered. "Holy hell," she croaked.

He reached out, rubbing a circle on her back, and leaned down until their faces were mere inches apart, her breath warming his lips as his cock stirred in his jeans. "Next time, maybe you should just listen to me. Believe me, if I wanted to make you gasp in my company, I'd do something else entirely."

Sadie lifted her gaze to his, hers heating in a split second. He could get lost in her eyes, those deep blue pools, especially now when they were heavy-lidded and hazy. Like she was thinking of all the utterly indecent things they'd done over the past week. All the things that had been running through his mind on a near-constant loop.

When he was this close to her, it was easy to forget about the townsfolk bustling around them. To feel like they were the only two people in the world and forget about all the reasons their being together was a bad idea.

The scary part was, the last time Cole had felt like that, he'd gotten lost in it and made the biggest mistake of his life.

CHAPTER 14

After swinging by The Willow Tree's outdoor booth and sweet-talking Finn into adjusting the alcohol ratio in their festive hot chocolates, Sadie and Cole strolled along the not-so-quiet streets, their shoulders brushing with every step. Every graze had Sadie's nerve endings firing, her breath catching as easily as a middle schooler holding hands with a boy for the first time.

She didn't know if it was the evidence Nat and Asher had given that Cole wasn't all bad, or finally seeing him outside the bedroom, proof that he was a complex human being—complete with a family who ribbed him—or the still extremely potent drink, but somewhere along the way tonight, she'd started to view him as someone more than the aloof, intimidating, irritatingly handsome man she'd boxed him into for years. More than the giant *nope* she'd stamped on him from the moment they'd met in front of the courthouse.

"A little birdie told me you're doin' work at the shelter now. How come you didn't tell me last night?" Last night, when he'd taken off her panties with his teeth before she'd ridden him on the chair in his suite. She could still feel his groans vibrating against her skin. Could still feel his fingers digging into her flesh.

His eyebrows lifted the tiniest bit, his only tell that she'd surprised him. "That little birdie works fast..."

"Usually does in Havenbrook."

"Maybe so. But regardless of small-town gossip, I don't talk about any of my clients. Attorney-client privilege."

She rolled her eyes. "I'm not askin' for details. I was just surprised, is all."

"Surprised because of how you've perceived me since your sister's divorce?"

She cringed before draining the last of her beverage and tossing the cup in the trash can, Cole's falling in just after hers. There was no denying she'd judged him by one act and one act alone, and how fair was that? She would hate it if the tables had been turned. "I had that comin'."

He shrugged. "It's not who I am, Sadie. It's just something I do."

And that something had suddenly become multifaceted, painting him in a whole new light. Recalibrating her preconceived notions and adjusting how she viewed him. How she'd *been* viewing him.

They walked in silence for long moments as Sadie wondered what else she'd gotten wrong about him. What else about himself had he kept hidden from her? But suddenly, she wasn't so sure she wanted to know. Already, she was teetering dangerously close to the edge, and one light touch could send her careening into the unknown with a man she knew was risky.

"You don't have to stick around, you know," she said finally, just to see what he would say. Would he stay with her, even after given an out? Did he *want* to?

He tilted his head to the side as he stared down at her. "Why wouldn't I?"

She lifted a shoulder and moved her attention back to their path. "You've never attended this before. If you're hangin' around just to make sure I'm okay, it's unnecessary. I can get back to the inn on my own."

He was quiet so long, she finally glanced up at him, their gazes locking immediately. His eyes bored into hers, a delicious weight settling over her skin, making her want to lean into him. To wrap her hand around the back of his neck and pull his face to hers. Press their lips together and remind herself exactly how delicious he tasted. Get lost in his groans and the hungry way he always seemed to grip her body, as if he couldn't get enough.

"How do you know I've never gone before?" he asked, his voice low and rough.

Well, hell. Because she was, apparently, a stalker. She'd kept tabs on him since he'd moved to Havenbrook, but she'd done so in order to help her sister avoid a run-in with him. Hadn't she? True, Elise had never once inferred a dislike of Cole, nor had she ever vocalized any sort of animosity, but sometimes a twin just knew what the other needed.

She shrugged. "I've never seen you at the inn during the event. But maybe that has less to do with the event and more to do with Starlight. Maybe you just don't like it there."

"If I didn't like Starlight Haven, would I have chosen it as a place to spend three weeks of my life?"

Well, that was a question she hadn't actually considered... And why the hell hadn't she? True, Havenbrook wasn't exactly a bustling metropolis, but there were more lodging options available than just Starlight. Of course, hers was the best—in her completely unbiased opinion. Also the nicest. And a man like Cole Donovan certainly enjoyed the finer things in life. That had to be all there was to it, right?

"Why did you?" she finally asked, desperate, for some reason, to know his answer. She glanced over in time to see his jaw tighten, the only whisper of emotion he allowed. He was very good at hiding them, but she'd been watching him enough that she could read those small tics. Could tell as soon as he walked into the inn what kind of a day he'd had and what she was in for that evening when they'd retreat to his room and spend the night wrapped in each other.

"You don't seem like the kind of woman who'd fish for compliments, Sadie."

She breathed out a laugh. "And if I were, I certainly wouldn't fish for them from you."

Although, he'd paid her compliments before, hadn't he? Nightly, when his eyes were hazy with lust, his lips hovering over her skin, parted as if trying to inhale her taste. That first night they'd slept together, he'd told her she was gorgeous. Breathtaking. Beautiful. And he'd managed to whisper similar words of adoration every night since.

"In that case, and in the interest of throwin' you off your game, I'll tell you that Starlight is the best in Havenbrook. It's the nicest with the longest list of amenities."

"That's true. But is that the only reason you picked it?"

He tugged her to a stop, his hand holding her own, heat zipping along her skin at the contact. When a family walked by, he stepped closer to her, their bodies now nearly flush, and Sadie wanted nothing more than to fall into him. To lift up on her toes and press their lips together. Kiss him with everyone in town as witness. "Were you hopin' I'd tell you something else? Something like how much I enjoy the fresh-baked cookies in the afternoon or the muffins delivered to my room each mornin'? Or that I find the woman who runs it unbelievably—"

"Y'all're still out here?" Edna slipped an arm through Sadie's and bumped their hips together, not so subtly shoving her into Cole.

"Whoa, easy." Cole steadied Sadie with firm but gentle hands on her hips. And though she might be wearing layers upon layers of clothes, she still felt the touch as sure as a brand against her skin. "You okay?" he asked low, his words just a whisper against her ear, the same tone and cadence he used when he settled his thick length deep inside her.

She shuddered and nodded, ignoring the tightening of her nipples and trying not to dwell on what the rest of Cole's sentence might've been before Edna interrupted.

Clearing her throat, she eyed the older woman. "What're *you* still doin' out here? Did you talk Finn into givin' you a drink after all?"

"Can't hide a thing from you, can I?" Edna grinned, all mischief and mayhem. She'd been scheming since well before Sadie was even born, and she pitied the poor fool who was Edna's next victim. "I was actually out lookin' for Mac. You seen your cousin around here anywhere?"

Sadie shook her head. "No, I haven't." Actually, she hadn't seen her cousin Mackenna in quite a while—not since her job duties had turned her life upside down. "Was she here tonight?"

"She was supposed to meet me for a carriage ride, and Fred's over there waitin'."

Sadie furrowed her brow. "You and...Mac...were gonna go on a horse-drawn carriage ride?" she asked, unable to suppress the skepticism in her voice.

"Yes, sugar. What's wrong with that?"

"Nothing," Sadie said quickly. "Not a thing. I'm sure friends enjoy it all the time." None that Sadie had ever seen, considering how romantic the ride was—or so her guests always told her—but who was she to judge?

"My thoughts exactly. But my friend bailed on me, so why don't y'all go on and enjoy it? Fred can bring you back to the inn since there's a nip in the air. Feels like snow's comin'."

"Oh no. No, that's fine. We're fine. We'll just—"

"Nonsense. It's right here, and it's already been paid for. You wouldn't want me to waste my money, would you, sugar?"

"No, of course not, but—"

"Then y'all go on and use it. I won't take no for an answer."

Somehow, without Sadie noticing, Edna had maneuvered them toward the horse-drawn carriage and now not so subtly shoved Sadie in that direction.

Fred, the coachman, lifted his top hat at their approach and stood. "Give me a sec. I'll be right down to help y'all up."

"I got it," Cole said as he gripped Sadie's waist and lifted her into the carriage as easily as if she weighed nothing more than a sack of flour. To be clear, she *definitely* weighed more than a sack of flour.

Sadie squeaked in surprise, spinning around in time to see Cole slip Edna some cash before climbing into the carriage alongside her.

She glanced between him and Edna, who strolled away with a grin on her face. "Did you just give her money?"

Cole lifted a single shoulder as he sat, pulling her along with him and settling her flush against his side, draping the thick wool blanket across their laps. "Didn't seem right that she paid for this when we're gonna enjoy it."

She narrowed her eyes at him and ignored the flip of her stomach. "Did y'all plan this?"

"Sadie, if you haven't learned by now that I'm neither that subtle nor that romantic, then you haven't been payin' attention." He placed his arm along the back of their seat, the warmth of his body seeping into her even through the layers separating them. He leaned down so their faces were merely inches apart, their breath intermingling in clouds between them. He smelled like chocolate and peppermint, like Christmas and winter nights, and she wanted to melt into him. To lay her hand against his stomach and press their lips together. To enjoy this ride as if it were truly a romantic date. "If I want something, I just come out and say it."

Caught in the magnetic pull of his gaze, she leaned closer to him, unable to stop herself. When she was a mere breath away, her eyelids drifted shut as Cole wrapped a hand around her head, his fingers delving into her hair. He held her jaw, tipping her face up to meet his, before lowering his mouth to hers. He groaned into the kiss, and Sadie barely held back her gasped surprise at the contact. They were still in the middle of town, seated up on a pedestal for everyone to see, and he was kissing the breath from her. He swiped his tongue against hers, and she reveled in the contact, inching her hand along his thigh under the blanket until she cupped his hard length and smiled as he groaned into her mouth.

"You're not playin' fair, firecracker."

"Who said I had to play fair?"

He leaned down until his mouth brushed her ear, ghosting his lower lip along the sensitive skin. "Just so we're clear, if you weren't wearin' jeans, I'd already have my fingers deep inside that perfect pussy. I'd make you come before we got back to the inn, too, wouldn't I? Because I know exactly how you like it."

She shuddered as he pressed his hand to the seam of her jeans, teasing her swollen clit with his words and light touches that would never get her off. "Why do you do this to me?"

"Because you love it."

There was no denying that. No denying how much she'd come to crave this man in such a short while. She just had no idea if he felt the same, but maybe this was the sign she'd needed. He'd kissed her for all the town to see, wrapped his arm around her and tugged her into his side. Whispered filthy words in her ear as the townsfolk looked on, unaware of the path his hand took beneath the blanket.

Maybe she could come like this, fully clothed, with a man old enough to be her grandfather guiding their path mere feet away.

But suddenly, Cole slowed his ministrations and whispered, "Open your eyes."

Hesitantly, she complied, blinking until their surroundings came into focus. She'd been so caught up in him, she hadn't even taken in how beautiful it was, sitting up here as they rolled through Havenbrook.

"Wow," she whispered, still tucked into his side.

The carriage itself was a winter wonderland masterpiece, the jingle of the sleigh bells strung from the reins intermingling with the clip-clop of the horses' hooves on the pavement. It was wrapped in garland and glittered with white lights that arched in a canopy above their heads. That only added to the magic of the experience as they rolled through the most festive streets in town, lit up for their pleasure.

"I've booked so many of these for other people, but I've never actually taken my own ride."

He pressed his lips to the crown of her head. "I should've paid Edna more, then."

She breathed out a laugh. "Yeah, I'll have to thank her."

What Sadie didn't say was that she'd love to be in a relationship with someone who thought to arrange things like this for her, just because they knew it'd make her happy. A picnic in a meadow, wine under the fireworks, or a romantic carriage ride during the holidays.

As they took in their surroundings during their slow ride back to Starlight, tiny specks of white fluff floated down around them, and a smile split her face. It didn't snow every year, but that only made it all the more special when it did.

She looked up at Cole, who was watching her instead of their surroundings, his eyes locked on her face as she basked in the snowflakes that'd never last. And even though she knew they'd be gone in the blink of an eye, that didn't mean she couldn't enjoy them for however long they stayed.

"Y'all wanna be dropped off at the main house?" Fred asked, breaking her out of her trance.

Cole squeezed her leg under the blanket, his thumb brushing over the seam along her inner thigh. "You need to check on things before you head back to the cottage for the night?"

"Um...y-yeah," she stammered, trying to recall if she'd mentioned earlier in the night needing to do either of those things, or if she was just that predictable.

He nodded once. Then, without ever taking his eyes from her, he said, "That'd be great, Fred. Thanks."

"No problem. Here we are." Fred pulled the reins, halting the horses in front of the path leading to the inn. "I've got a stool for y'all. Let me grab it to help Miss Sadie climb down safely."

"We're all right." Cole tossed the blanket aside and jumped down from the carriage before turning to face her.

Glancing down at the drop to the ground, Sadie snorted and stood. "Speak for yourself. I'm too short and out of shape to jump and land gracefully."

"I wouldn't let you fall." He lifted his hands to her, resting them on her waist, his eyebrow cocked in question. "May I?"

Placing her hands on his shoulders, she gave a subtle nod and held her breath as he lifted her out of the carriage and set her down directly in front of him, their bodies brushing along the way. He was still hard, the length of him pressing into her and making her ache with need. They were so close, his exhales fluttered wisps of her hair around her face. It'd be all too easy to press up on her tiptoes, tug his face down toward hers, and kiss him again. Lose herself in his touch and his taste and the feel of his body against hers.

Cole reached up and brushed his thumb across the apple of her cheek, his warm touch against her chilled skin sending a shudder through her. "Snowflake," he murmured, his gaze dropping from her eyes to her lips, and then he did exactly what she'd hoped he would.

He lowered his head and stole her breath, his tongue swiping against her lower lip as he gripped her ass, having no concern at all for who might be watching. And, in that moment, Sadie didn't either. She couldn't remember why being with him wasn't the smartest thing, especially when he made her feel like this. As if a bottle of champagne had opened inside her chest, all bubbly and warm, and coated every inch of her.

"Y'all have a great night," Fred called, snapping the reins as he rode off.

"C'mon, let's get you inside," Cole murmured against her lips before pulling back. He linked their fingers together, pulling her behind him as he climbed the front porch steps, entered the code on the door, and held it open for her.

"Thanks," she murmured, ignoring how her nipples peaked as she slid past him. Ignoring, too, all the questions this evening had brought up. Like what the hell they were doing now. She'd had an answer for that before tonight—they'd been bed partners. *Fantastic* bed partners, but that was where it ended. Tonight, though... Tonight changed things, didn't it?

As soon as they stepped over the threshold, they nearly ran into Elise, who had very obviously been waiting for Sadie to arrive. "I'm out," she said, barely sparing Cole—or his and Sadie's linked hands—a glance as she slipped into her coat.

"Wait," Sadie said. "How'd it go tonight?"

Elise shrugged, one hand on the doorknob. "Fine. Busy. We ran out of your muffins around 8:30, but I plied the rest of the freeloaders with wine."

"Really? That's great!" Sadie said as Cole squeezed her hand. She'd prepared as many muffins as last year, plus about twenty-five percent extra, which meant they'd seen quite a bit more traffic. "And how about—"

Elise held up a hand before Sadie could finish. "Everyone's already in for the night, so we're both free." She blew through the front door and lifted a hand in a wave. "See you tomorrow."

"Bye," Sadie said, although her sister was already gone. She couldn't blame her for her hasty retreat—working the Sip and Shop was extremely demanding, and Sadie was always exhausted at the end of the evening.

"Well..." She turned to face Cole, their fingers still linked between them. "It looks like I'm free for the rest of the night."

"Looks like."

"Thanks for tonight." She glanced down at their hands

and took a deep breath before lifting her gaze to his. "I can't believe I'm sayin' this, but I had fun."

Cole cocked a brow. "Quite the compliment comin' from you."

She pressed a hand into his stomach and shoved lightly. "You know what I mean..."

"Yeah. Who'd have thought we could be in the same proximity without either bitin' each other's heads off or rippin' each other's clothes off?" His gaze dropped briefly to Sadie's lips, then her breasts, which were very interested in the attention, before tipping his head toward the back door. "C'mon, I'll walk you to the cottage."

Every night this week, they'd retreated to his suite at the end of her day and proceeded to spend hours wrapped up in each other. But maybe this sort-of date had been enough to scare him off.

She breathed out a laugh, even as disappointment swept over her. "It's twenty feet away, in our fenced backyard," she said. "And I make this trek nearly every night."

"And I watch you from the door every night, so this isn't much different. Just humor me." He held open the back door for her, gesturing her to walk through first.

"You don't need to worry about me. I've taken self-defense. My cousin Mac taught me. I can handle myself."

"Of that, I have no doubt." But he still didn't let go of her hand. Still didn't stop his gaze from tracking their surroundings, no doubt looking for any threat, which was utterly laughable.

They stepped onto her tiny front porch, and she used

the keypad to unlock her front door before pushing it open. He still hadn't let go of her hand. Hadn't stepped back. Hadn't made an excuse to leave.

Turning around to face him, she asked, "Why'd you feel the need to walk me back here?"

He brushed his thumb against the back of her hand. "You remember what I said durin' the carriage ride?"

"You said a lot of things. What item, in particular, are you referrin' to?"

"I said I'm not subtle. If I want something, I come out and say it."

"Yeah, I remember." She dropped her gaze to his lips, her body humming at the thought of those on any part of her tonight. "Any reason you're bringin' that up right now while you're standin' on my front step? You wouldn't be anglin' for an invite in, would you?"

"I'm not anglin' for anything, firecracker." He placed his hand on her hip beneath her jacket, his thumb tucked under her sweater, brushing maddeningly against her skin. "I'm sayin' I wanna come inside. I'm sayin' I wanna strip you naked and fuck you over the arm of that couch. I'm sayin' I want you to sit on my face until you come all over my tongue and I can still taste you in the mornin'." He ducked his head into the crook of her neck, sweeping his lips against her sensitive skin, flicking his tongue out to lick at her pulse point. "I'm sayin' I wanna hear you scream my name inside these walls."

She swallowed hard, her clit throbbing from his words

alone as she tilted her head and allowed him more access. "That's...that's an awful lot to live up to in one night."

"Maybe, but you've been with me enough times that you know I'll make good on every single promise." He kissed a path up her neck and along her jaw until their lips brushed with his every word. "What do you say, fire-cracker? You gonna invite me in?"

Instead of answering with words, she gripped his coat and tugged him inside, shutting the door behind them. Cole might not be hers for forever, but, just like the snow, she intended to enjoy whatever time they had together while it lasted.

CHAPTER 15

Cole was in trouble. He'd known it from the second he'd run into Sadie in the Square, and the more time they spent together, the less doubt he had. But now? Following her into her pseudo home with the false intention that he simply wanted to fuck her? He was in deeper than even he'd realized. Because while, yes, he definitely did want to spend as much time as possible between her legs, that wasn't the only reason he'd invited himself in.

He just wasn't ready to say goodnight. He didn't want their time together to end. And wasn't that just a kick in the nuts?

As Sadie slipped out of those fuck me boots, he took a cursory glance around the space. It was small but open, the single room housing a sofa and coffee table, a bed, and a kitchenette, with a door leading to what he assumed was the bathroom.

He tossed off his coat and then stalked toward her where she stood in front of the couch. "Which first?" he asked, peeling her jacket from her shoulders and tossing it to the side.

"What do you mean?"

"Did you forget already, firecracker? I told you I wanted to fuck you over the arm of the couch and have you ridin' my face. Now I just need to know what you want first."

"Maybe I don't want to do either of those things," Sadie said, lifting her arms for him as he removed her sweater.

"I don't know who you're tryin' to fool, but it sure as hell isn't me." He reached around and unhooked her bra, freeing her gorgeous tits and making his hands ache to cup them, but he restrained himself, instead sliding his fingers down to work on her jeans. "I'm the one who's been standin' behind you as you've ridden that sweet pussy back on my cock with no help from me." He sat on the couch and lowered her jeans and panties until she could step out of them. Until she stood in front of him wearing nothing but a flush. "And I'm the one who can still taste you every mornin' because neither of us can go a single night without my tongue lickin' up all your sweetness. So, I'm gonna ask you again—which do you want buried inside you first? My cock or my tongue?"

She stood there for a moment, her bottom lip caught between her teeth, her nipples stiff peaks and her eyes heavy-lidded as she stared down at him. Finally, she said, "Your tongue."

With a satisfied smirk, he reached back and tugged at the neck of his sweater, pulling it off with a quick yank. Then he slid off the couch and onto the floor, adjusting his head back on the cushions so she could rest her knees there. He smacked her ass hard enough to jerk her forward. "Then climb on up here, firecracker, and ride it."

"Some people might consider your bossiness a turn-off. Do you know that?"

"What I know is you aren't one of those people." He groaned as she got into position, her soaked pussy hovering over his face and making his mouth water. "Look at how wet you are, just from my bossy ass. Fucking gorgeous. Now hold on, baby. This is gonna be quick."

He reached up and cupped her ass in both palms, bringing her closer to his mouth, and then he went in for the kill. Sadie loved when he feasted on her, and he happened to fucking crave it, so he was no stranger to this and knew exactly what she needed to get off as fast as possible. And it was going to be fast. Because the need to be inside her beat like a drum within his chest, urging him to sink deep. To get as close to her as he possibly could in the only way that was safe for him—with his body.

"*Cole*," she said, panting and gripping the back of the couch, her hips rocking against his face as he delved his tongue between her folds.

He hummed in response, and she gasped, just like he

knew she would. Gripping her ass, he tugged her cheeks apart, the tip of one finger brushing lightly against her back entrance, and Sadie shuddered at the contact.

Pulling back, he blew against her clit, keeping his finger right where it was. "You like that, dirty girl?"

"No, I—"

"You sure?" he asked, this time swiping the area with intent.

Sadie sobbed out a moan as she ground down harder against him. "Oh God, don't stop. Don't stop, don't—*Cole*."

He slipped just the tip of his finger inside, and she went off like a rocket, moaning his name as she came on his tongue, her hips rocking against his face. He licked up every bit of her, sucking her lips between his, getting drunk on her taste.

Fuck, how could he be this addicted to her in such a short period of time? It was becoming a compulsion, but one he wasn't inclined to work on. No, what he was inclined to work on was getting them as close as two people possibly could, seeing how many times he could make her come in one night, and ruining her for all other men. Because if he couldn't have her for forever, he sure as hell wanted to make sure she remembered him that long.

He slid out from under her and reached into his pocket, pulling out a condom. Ripping it open before rolling it down his shaft, he feasted his eyes on her. She still gripped the back of the couch, her head hanging loosely between her shoulders, her panting breaths ringing in the room. She was spent but still needy, her legs spread and pussy wet and waiting for him.

"I already made you come, but you still need something, don't you, firecracker? Tell me. Tell me what you need."

She glanced at him over her shoulder. "I didn't think your ego was what I'd be strokin' tonight."

He knelt on the couch behind her, shifting her so she braced her hands on the arm, and swept the head of his cock through her slit. "My ego got stroked plenty when you moaned my name with my tongue in your pussy. But yet you're still sittin' here, your legs spread and waitin' for something, and I just wanna make sure I give you what you're hopin' for."

Actually, he wanted to hear her say it—*needed* to—just so he didn't feel so alone in this. Because Christ knew he needed every goddamn ounce of her, from her sharp tongue to her infectious laugh and hopeful outlook and giving heart.

She stared at him, her eyes heavy with desire and need. "I want you inside me. Just like you promised. Unless you don't think you can make me come again..."

He huffed out a laugh, smirking as he rested his hand on her upturned ass before swatting it sharply. "There must be a reason you're antagonizin' me. Someone wants to get fucked hard."

Unable to spend another second without the welcoming heat of her pussy surrounding him, he sank deep in one thrust, their groans mingling in the air.

"Christ, Sadie. I'm never gonna get tired of this. Not as long as I fucking live. I crave how your pussy sucks me in deep and those throaty little moans I fuck out of your throat and how you whimper my name when you're gettin' close. And I get you close, don't I? Every damn time."

"*Yes*. So close."

He bent over her, kissing a trail across her shoulders as he palmed her tits, tweaking her nipples between his fingers. Brushing his lips against her ear, he said, "Tell me I'm the only one who's made you feel like this. Tell me no one knows this body like I do."

"You," she managed through panting breaths, reaching back to cup his neck. "It's just you."

Those words set off something inside him, and he pumped into her faster, an unrelenting urge coursing through him to take and claim. To *keep*.

It wasn't the first time that instinct had hit him, and he feared the more time he spent with her, the louder that whisper would grow until it was a roar.

"C'mon, firecracker, let me feel you come. Squeeze my cock and show it who owns me."

She turned her head toward him, her lips parted and resting on his, their eyes connected as he thrust into her over and over. Wanting desperately to lose himself inside her because he knew this was the one place he'd be found.

"Cole, I— I—" She moaned as she came, her pussy tightening enough to stutter his thrusts, and he had no chance of holding on any longer.

He sank deep, gripping her tightly to him as he fell over the edge with her.

And it was then, with Sadie's eyes on his, their bodies locked together, her scent filling his nose and her taste still on his tongue, that Cole worried he was already in too deep. Worried he'd already fallen. He could only hope it wouldn't kill him when it inevitably came to an end.

CHAPTER 16

Cole woke up the following morning and blinked into the unfamiliar room. It took him a moment to realize he was in Sadie's bed. Instinctively, he reached out, searching for her, but her side was cold.

It'd been so long since he'd done this whole morning-after thing. In fact, he'd...never done it. He and Amber had been high school sweethearts, so there'd never been an awkward morning after. And since his divorce, he'd never put himself in any situations where he might get attached —like staying the night with someone. He had no idea what had come over him last night to make him stay.

But...no. That wasn't true. He knew *exactly* what had come over him. Sadie. She'd wormed her way inside, despite all the ways he'd held himself apart and closed himself off. And now what the fuck was he supposed to do?

He threw off the covers and climbed out of bed,

171

uncaring of his nakedness as he collected his articles of clothing they'd strewn across the cottage the night before. Reminding him exactly how they'd spent the evening. How she'd shaken in his arms, her body clenching around him as she'd begged for more. Begged for *him*.

"Fuck," he mumbled, scrubbing a hand over his face as he diligently ignored his erection that seemed to be ever-present with thoughts of Sadie.

While there was no doubt he'd wanted to do all of those things to her, he couldn't deny that he'd said them to hide his need to be with her last night. He'd done so in order to distance himself from what he was powerless to stop from happening between them. A hell of a lot of good that had done him.

Each time they'd slept together, he'd fallen a little bit more for her. How could he not? Sadie was gorgeous and intelligent, selfless and loyal, kind and funny. He loved that she wasn't afraid to put him in his place. Loved that she challenged him every second she was in his presence. Wasn't timid or shy about giving it as good as she got—at least, not with him.

There certainly wasn't anything timid or shy about their attraction to each other. He'd never, in all of his thirty-three years, experienced this kind of explosive chemistry. It was intoxicating and had to be why she was on his mind constantly. He couldn't fall asleep without thinking about her, couldn't wake up without her face being the first thing he saw in his mind, couldn't talk to his sister or his momma without wondering if they'd like her as much as he did.

And that thought scared the hell out of him. He'd lost himself once to love. Had fallen down a rabbit hole of coupledom, where even their names couldn't be said separately. After the divorce, he'd had to learn at twenty-nine how to be his own person. Years later, he was finally starting to like who he'd turned into, who he'd become. And he refused to box himself into another codependent relationship with someone dead set on controlling his every move.

Ignoring the voice in his head that reminded him Sadie hadn't attempted to do that, he reached for his jeans hanging over the back of the couch and tugged them on, finding a scrap of paper tucked into the pocket. With a furrowed brow, he pulled it out and unfolded it, running his eyes over the loopy script.

I had to run and start breakfast for the inn and didn't want to wake you. Make yourself at home. Feel free to use the shower and help yourself to whatever. The door locks on its own, so you don't have to worry about that. Thanks for last night. xo, Sadie

He ignored the way his gut tightened, same as his chest, at how familiar this all felt. How *terrifying*. He hadn't let anyone in since his ex-wife. Hadn't wanted to. He'd been happy on his own, figuring out his shit. Being the man he wanted to be and not some version of someone else's ideal. He'd had no intention of complicating that.

And then, three years ago and only months after his divorce, Sadie had come along and knocked him on his proverbial ass. Even from afar, he'd been drawn to her. Had felt it like a tug under his skin, as if they were magnets drawn to each other. And that pull had only intensified over time. Had intensified to the point of bursting when he'd picked Starlight Haven to stay during his renovations.

"You're a fucking idiot," he mumbled to himself, pulling on his jacket and strolling out the cottage's front door without a backward glance.

If he had no intention of entering into a relationship with her, why the hell had he started something? Why the hell had he spent his nights getting lost in her body? Spent the actual night wrapped around her, her curves settling perfectly against his body? He'd known from the beginning she was a commitment girl down to her bones. She wanted a happy ending for herself, and he'd already watched his first marriage crumble. He had absolutely no desire to put himself through that again simply for a chance this one might stick.

Using the code Sadie had given him several days ago, he unlocked the back door and strode through the inn, intent on getting to his room and washing off last night, along with the emotions it had conjured up that were suddenly crackling under his skin.

He heard Sadie's voice before he saw her, the sound like honey coating his insides, all warm and sweet. He rounded a corner and stopped abruptly as soon as she came into view. She stood behind the front desk, her hair a chaos of waves around her face and a man he'd never seen before leaning too close to her for anyone who wasn't an invited guest in her bed.

"I was thinkin' maybe you'd finally be able to show me around," the man said. "Try out that restaurant you've been tellin' me about."

Cole tightened his hands into fists at his sides, anger and irritation rearing their heads inside him so quickly, he barely had time to process it before he strode toward them. Didn't even bother to remove what was no doubt a murderous expression written on his face, but he'd be damned if he let this fucker hit on the woman he'd been inside just hours before.

"I'll be happy to get you a reservation there, but I don't think my boyfriend would like it too much if we went out," Sadie said, her tone friendly but firm.

Cole's steps faltered. *Boyfriend?* Was that what last night meant to her? Jesus, he'd really fucked up if that was the case. He'd put the needs of his cock over her feelings, and now he was faced with a situation he'd never intended to be in again.

She lifted her gaze to him, the tension immediately seeping out of her features as relief replaced it, and he ignored the urge to comfort her. To cup her face and crash his lips down against hers. Let this jackass know who she belonged to.

He ignored it because it was absolutely fucking crazy. She didn't belong to anyone, least of all him.

"Hey, baby," she said, the tiniest hint of apprehension bleeding into her voice, and he pretended his chest didn't tighten at the endearment falling from her lips. "You sleep all right last night?" Her tone was stilted, her eyes pleading as she stared up at him, attempting to communicate something. Gone was the taunting lilt he was so accustomed to hearing from her, the one he loved so much, and in its place was this saccharine tone she'd never used on him before.

"Fine." He stopped himself a mere foot behind the jackass, and the other man stood upright sharply, knocking over the cup of pens on the desk as he whirled around to face Cole.

"Oh, oh... Uh, excuse me." The man scurried off without another glance toward Sadie as Cole glared at his retreating form.

He had no idea why he felt this burning jealousy deep in his gut or where it had come from. He'd never been jealous with his ex-wife, even though he'd very obviously had good reason to be. He didn't know if this emotion was innate in him, and something Amber had just never managed to tap, or if it was only Sadie who brought it out.

Regardless of why it was there, he needed to shove it down deep and never speak of it again. Needed to ignore it entirely, because Sadie wasn't his, and he had no right to feel this sort of possession over her. They didn't have a commitment to each other. If she wanted to go out with that guy—or any guy, for that matter—she could. Cole couldn't do anything to stop her.

And he hated the very fucking thought of it.

COLE HAD HAD AN ABSOLUTELY shit day. He'd tried to shove his morning out of his mind, tried to shove *Sadie* out of his mind, but it'd been no use. He'd spent the entire day with his head in his ass, thoughts of her and their interactions overtaking his attention when it should've been on Jemma's case.

This was getting out of hand. He'd had to come into the office on a Sunday, for fuck's sake, because he'd spent half of the prior week imagining Sadie spread out on his desk. This was beginning to affect his career and the level of work he was producing for his clients. He'd had to redirect his focus more times than he'd care to admit, and when he typically worked in billable hours—Jemma's case notwithstanding—that meant it was not only costing him his sanity, but also his time and money.

All he wanted to do was go home. Back to his house where he didn't have to interact with anyone. Where he could open a beer, veg in front of the TV, and do absolutely nothing. Instead, he had to go back to his temporary home at Starlight Haven—the place he'd begun to view as the root cause of all this. Maybe if he'd chosen one of the other options in Havenbrook, none of this ever would've happened.

Was that what he wanted, though? Even though Sadie was causing disruption in his life, he couldn't say he'd take a different path if he had the opportunity to do it over again. True, if he hadn't picked Sadie's inn to stay at, then, more than likely, Nat wouldn't have found him and asked him to partner up with Sadie for the photography shoot, and thus, his life wouldn't have been thrown into chaos.

But then he also wouldn't know how she got that sparkle in her eyes when she was about to rib him or how kind she was, leaving notes on his plate of muffins each morning, or how hard she worked at her goals. He wouldn't know the tenor of her moans or how her thighs quivered when she was close to coming or exactly how she looked, her hair falling like fire around him, as she rode them both to climax.

Great, and now he was strolling into Starlight half hard courtesy of the woman behind the front desk. After his divorce, he swore that he'd never be tied down again. That he'd never commit himself to someone who wanted so much more from him than he could give. Who wanted him to be someone he wasn't. But it was times like this, when Sadie's smiling eyes fell on him, a tiny, playful quirk to her lips he swore was just for him, that he thought he might enjoy being tied down again, if he were tied to her.

"Hey," she said, sweeping her gaze over him before cocking an eyebrow. "Long day?"

He blew out a breath and ran a hand through his hair, not bothering to lower his messenger bag from his shoulder. "What, no crack about how I look like shit?"

"I figured I could give you a pass tonight, considerin' you spent an entire Sunday workin'. You don't seem to be on your game like usual."

"You could say that."

Despite the late hour, she didn't press him for any more details, didn't push him to tell her what the problem was, though the space between her eyebrows pinched slightly. "I didn't get a chance to tell you this mornin', but thanks for playin' along with that whole boyfriend thing. I've used the excuse before, but that guy won't take no for an answer. I'm just glad I had someone to point to this time."

Cole's jaw tightened, his teeth clenching over the thought of anyone harassing Sadie to the point where she had to utter, "He won't take no for an answer." "He's bothered you before?"

She rolled her eyes and waved a dismissive hand. "You don't have to get all growly about it. I can handle myself, but this is just easier. He's a businessman from Tennessee, and he's been comin' here once a month for about a year. I've always told him I have a boyfriend when he asks me out, but he doesn't care. So when you strolled in, I saw an opportunity to shut him down once and for all. I hope that's okay."

He ignored the part of him who *wanted* to be her excuse. Wanted to be the reason she said no to men who asked her out on dates. Wanted to be the reason she had that smile on her face. But he'd buried that part of himself years ago, and he had no intention of excavating it now.

"It's fine. Hopefully now, he'll leave you alone."

"Fingers crossed he gets the picture this week while he's here." She grinned at him, a teasing pull to those full lips he loved so much. "Don't worry, though, I won't ask you to the New Year's Eve ball or anything to prove it."

"No?" And just why the fuck did it bother him that she discounted him for an event he had absolutely no intention of attending, with or without her?

"Well, obviously not." She swiped a hand through the air as if the very thought of them together was preposterous, and he didn't know why that cut so deep. "You know what they say about a kiss at midnight."

"What's that?"

Her gaze dropped to his lips, and she wet her own. The tiny flick of her tongue against that pale pink flesh was enough to harden him completely, his cock a thick, throbbing nuisance behind his zipper. Christ, why could he never control himself around her?

When she spoke, her voice came out rough and low, just how it got after her first orgasm. "The person you kiss at midnight is who you intend to spend the rest of the year with. And we both know your feelings on commitment."

There it was, out in the open, impossible for either of them to ignore any longer. They'd had these differences the entirety of the time they'd known each other—both distantly and since he'd been staying at Starlight Haven—but they'd never specifically come out and said as much. Deniability wasn't an option anymore.

He dropped his bag to the floor and braced his hands

on the desk, meeting her eyes. "We do. Which begs the question...what're you doin' with me, Sadie?"

Her brows pinched as she regarded him. "What do you mean?"

"I mean...it's pretty obvious that I'm not right for you."

She swallowed and averted her gaze to the papers fanned out across the desk and gathered them before stacking them into a pile. "That's a bit presumptuous, don't you think? Who said I'd want you in the first place?"

He breathed out a laugh and shook his head. "Always with the smart mouth."

Lowering his gaze to her lips, he looked his fill, remembering when she'd dropped to her knees in his suite and sucked him deep the second time they'd been together. For as long as he stayed there, he'd see her in every corner of his room. Remember every piece of furniture he'd fucked her against. Every place he'd made her come.

Squeezing his eyes shut, he pressed his thumb and forefinger there, shaking his head. "Look," he breathed, forcing himself to meet her eyes as he ripped off the Band-Aid and got this over with so they could both move on. "The sex is fantastic. There's no denyin' that."

Her eyebrows hit her hairline even as scarlet brushed her cheeks. "Well... That's blunt. And an understatement."

"I don't know if this kind of chemistry is normal for you, but it's not for me."

She shook her head, tucking her hair behind her ear. "Me neither," she answered softly.

Christ, why did that make what he had to do even worse?

"Sex still isn't enough to build a relationship on, though."

"Who said anything about a relationship?"

"C'mon, Sadie. You and I both know you wouldn't be happy with anything less than that."

When her only response was to roll her lips between her teeth, he knew he had his answer. And he didn't realize until right then just how much he'd hoped for her denial, if only to stay with her a little longer.

He leaned forward, belatedly wishing he hadn't stood on the other side of the desk. If this was going to be the last time he had the chance to touch her, he wanted to *touch* her. Wanted to brush the hair away from her face, run his thumb over her lower lip, and memorize the texture. Wanted to lick his way inside and taste her once more.

"I like you, firecracker. A lot. I like how you challenge me and how you don't put up with anything from me. I like how you mouth off just for my reaction. And it's because of how much I like you that I think we should stop whatever this is between us before it goes too far. Settle into friendship now that you don't hate my guts anymore."

She pursed her lips as she watched him, then nodded. "Ah, lookin' out for me, are you? Since I obviously can't be trusted to make that decision on my own?"

Cole blew out a heavy sigh and shook his head. "You know that's not what I'm sayin'. If there's anyone who can handle themselves, it's you. But you can't deny how different we are. You've told me more times than I can remember how much you believe in that happy ending, and how much you want it." He met her eyes, ignoring the tightness in his chest, the irritating twist of his stomach. "I'm just not the guy to give it to you."

CHAPTER 17

W ell, Sadie certainly hadn't seen that plot twist coming. A permanent bachelor, the forever fuck buddy, growing a conscience and breaking things off before she got attached? *Ha*. Well, the joke was on him, because she was already attached. She had no idea when the hell that had happened in the mere week they'd spent together, but apparently it had.

But, actually, if she were honest with herself, she'd admit she'd been attached for quite some time. Since well before Cole had booked his stay at the inn. Well before their explosive photo session with Nat. Well before their first kiss or the first time they'd slept together. Well before he'd helped her at the inn, before they'd strolled the streets of Havenbrook together, and before their moonlit carriage ride.

She hadn't known what to expect when she fell in love for the first time, but she'd assumed it'd be gradual. A slow build into comfort and familiarity rather than the sudden drop of a roller coaster.

She'd fallen for Cole as a mixture of both. Felt a spark of connection the first time their eyes had met from across the Square, and even more so when they'd officially met, though she'd buried that down deep. Shoved it in the recesses of her mind and locked it up tight, never to be addressed again. But the trouble with love was it seeped out from every crack and crevice. Bled into your very soul, whether you wanted it to or not.

Somewhere in her subconscious, she must have known, must have realized exactly what was bound to happen between her and Cole. Which was why she'd flipped the switch to hate so very easily in the months and years following Elise's divorce.

And now, look where that had gotten her.

"What's with your face?" Elise asked from her perch on the sofa in the Starlight's main gathering space.

It was Christmas Eve, but when you managed an inn for a living, you didn't get days off. So, for the past three years, with their parents in Florida, they'd spent their evening in front of the fireplace, splayed out on the sofa and bingeing *Gilmore Girls'* Christmas episodes on the small laptop propped between them. Tomorrow, their aunt, Caroline Haven, would bring them a couple plates of home-cooked deliciousness, and Sadie would bake an apple pie. But for tonight, they'd gorge themselves on appetizers, get tipsy on hot buttered rum, and finally stumble into the cottage after midnight, all whispers and giggles.

They'd fall into bed and snuggle up together exactly how they'd slept for the first ten years of their lives.

"This is just my face." Sadie didn't bother to take her gaze off the current episode, *"Women of Questionable Morals."*

Because, well, Elise would be able to tell she was lying. And, well, Sadie hadn't told her sister about the breakup with Cole—if that was what you could even call it. Or, actually, about anything at all to do with Cole.

"Um, hello? We have the same face, and that is *not* my face." Elise sipped from her hot buttered rum and eyed Sadie over the rim of the mug. "So, what is it? You and Cole stop seein' each other?"

Sadie choked on absolutely nothing and proceeded to cough until tears streamed down her face and her sister offered her a halfhearted back-slap. Once she'd caught her breath, she managed a broken, "'scuse me?"

Elise rolled her eyes. "Oh, please. You're not that stealthy. I'm just shocked you finally let it happen, considerin' the stick permanently lodged up your ass."

"First of all, I do *not* have a stick permanently lodged up my ass. One of us has to be the responsible one, and you already called dibs on being the flaky one." When her sister only offered a shrug, Sadie continued, "And second, what you do mean 'finally let it happen'?"

"Your obsession with him, obviously."

Sadie huffed out an indignant sound. "I'm not *obsessed* with him."

"Fine then, whatever you wanna call bein' overly

aware of his every move and havin' an intense reaction to absolutely anything he did at all, even breathe."

"Oh yeah? Since when?" And by that, she meant since when had her sister been paying so much damn attention to what she did with regard to Cole?

"I don't know... When did he move in to town?" she said, as blandly as she'd comment on the weather forecast.

Sadie gasped. "You are not tryin' to say I've"—she *refused* to utter any variation of the word obsession in the same sentence as Cole—"been interested in Cole for more than three years."

"I'm not *tryin'* to do anything. I just am." Elise ran her gaze over Sadie from head to toe and back again, her lips twisted up in a smirk. "And three years, huh? Amazin' how you knew that right off the top of your head."

"I knew it because it was right around the time of your divorce, idiot." Ah yes, the sisterly love coming out right on time for the holiday. Sadie was surprised they'd made it past ten, actually. "Or have you forgotten about that and the role Cole had in it?"

This time, when Elise turned her gaze on Sadie, she brought her whole body along for the ride, twisting on her cushion so they could face each other, a confused pinch to her brows. "Wait... Does your whole ridiculous fake-hate thing have to do with the divorce?"

"It's not fake," she said adamantly, even though she was lying through her teeth. "And obviously."

"But...but...*why*? I didn't get divorced from Cole. He wasn't the jackass who cheated on me and then stole

Great-Grandma's antiques, only to shove them in a storage unit just so I couldn't have 'em."

"Well, no, but he was the jackass who made all that happen for Alec."

Elise rolled her eyes. "That's his job, Sadie. If a surgeon lost a patient on the operatin' table, would you call them a murderer?"

"Obviously not. You're bein' dramatic. That's not at all the same thing."

She lifted a single shoulder. "Whatever. I just think you hatin' on him for doin' his job is stupid, is all. And not worth your happiness."

"Who said I was happy?"

Elise breathed out a laugh and shook her head. "Twin, remember? I may not be around all the time to witness your every move, but I do see you every day. And there's no denyin' you've been less stick-assy the past few weeks."

"That's not a word," Sadie mumbled, feeling unsettled. Not because of what her sister said, but because it was true. She'd been more relaxed, more laid-back, and definitely happier since her first kiss with Cole. "Besides, it doesn't matter anyway. He called it off. Said we'd never work. He's right." She shrugged and forced out a laugh even as her eyes filled. "Who's ever heard of a wedding planner and a divorce attorney finding their happily ever after together anyway?"

"It could happen," Elise said softly.

"No, I really don't think it could. He's not my forever. He's not *anyone's* forever. He doesn't want to be."

Elise pressed her foot into Sadie's thigh—the most affection her sister would likely show—and Sadie pretended that was enough. That she was fine, sitting there on Christmas Eve, the man her heart had somehow attached itself to sleeping right down the hall, even when it felt like everything she'd ever wanted was slipping through her fingers. And she had no idea how to stop it.

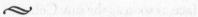

COLE HAD no fucking idea how one tiny firecracker of a woman could have demolished him so completely in such a short amount of time. Yet there he was, driving thirty miles to Forest Falls an hour before midnight on New Year's Eve, just so he wasn't tempted to show up at the ball and kiss Sadie despite knowing better.

He'd tried forcing her out of his mind in the week since he'd moved out of Starlight Haven and back to his newly remodeled house. A place that somehow, over the course of a month, had turned sterile and cold. It hadn't been until his third day home that he'd realized it wasn't the surroundings that were so cold, but rather the lack of Sadie in them.

Blowing out a frustrated breath, he pulled up in front of his momma's and sister's houses, seeing the lights on in Carly's, and headed that way. He knocked twice and opened the door without waiting for an answer, stepping over the threshold and listening for sounds from inside.

After mere seconds, his sister popped her head around

the corner, baseball bat in her hand and a murderous expression on her face. As soon as she saw him, she dropped the weapon to her side, her eyebrows flying up her forehead as she glanced behind him and then met his gaze with a furrowed brow. "Cole? What're you doin' here so late?"

"My baby's home?" his momma called from the kitchen before joining Carly, a smile sweeping across her face as soon as she saw Cole.

She held her arms open and strode toward him, happiness written all over her beautiful face. In her midfifties, Charlotte Donovan was still stunning, her kindness shining through in her eyes and her smile, her blond hair now leaning more toward gray.

He bent down and wrapped his arms around her, breathing in her familiar scent. "Hey, Momma."

She pulled back, holding him at arm's length as she frowned up at him. "What's that tone all about?"

He forced out a laugh and shook his head. "I said two words to you. How could you infer a tone from that?"

"A momma knows these things."

"Your sister can tell too," Carly said with a pointed stare.

He followed them into the kitchen, where it looked like they'd had a party based on the plethora of snacks spread across the counter. "What the hell happened in here?"

"Better question," his sister said, looking at him with a raised eyebrow, "is why are *you* here this late on New Year's Eve—without Sadie, no less."

He ignored the sharp stab in his gut at her name and settled into a chair at the dining room table. "How do you even remember her name? You met her for five minutes."

"It may only have been five minutes, but it was long enough for her to tell me about it," his mom said.

"Great," he grumbled. "Thanks for that. You always were a snitch."

Carly laughed without shame and sat down in the chair across from him, their mom taking a seat at the head of the table. "Maybe so, but I'm not wrong, am I?"

"Not wrong about what?"

"You like her. More than like her."

Yeah, he did. He'd spent the better portion of his time away from her denying it, but he figured there wasn't a point to that anymore.

"It doesn't matter. I'm not the kind of man she's lookin' for."

"Well, I don't believe that for a second. And if it's true, you don't want her anyway," his mom said, a sharp edge to her voice.

Carly rolled her eyes. "It's not true. She's totally and completely into him. I saw it with my own eyes. He's just being an idiot. And a stubborn ass."

"I'm so glad I decided to make the drive out here to ring in the new year with you both," he said dryly.

His sister laughed. "No, you're not. Which begs the question, why *did* you come? How'd you screw it up with her?"

"I didn't screw it up. I did what I needed to and called it off."

"Why the hell would you do that?"

He sighed and braced his elbows on the table, scrubbing his hands over his face. "Not that it's any of your business, but we're too different. I can't give her what she needs."

"And what is it that she needs? Someone who'll care for her? Protect her and cherish her? Who'll laugh with her and challenge her?" she pressed. "Are you tellin' me you don't do any of those things?"

He opened his mouth to disagree before snapping it shut.

"That's what I thought," his sister said, not a little smug.

"I've already done this before, and we all know how well that worked out." Not only had he lost his wife, but he'd lost his best friend. The two relationships he'd thought he could count on.

His mom reached over and patted his hand. "Honey, you've done it before, yes. But you were too young, and you did it with the wrong person. We all knew it. Hell, you probably knew it too, but you ignored it, because you thought bein' together as long as y'all had been meant you needed to take that next step. You proposed out of obligation." She lifted her eyebrows in a *tell me I'm wrong* gesture, and when he didn't say anything, she continued, "From what Carly told me, this thing with Sadie is new.

And if you're feelin' like this about her after this short of a time, maybe that's something to think about, hmm?"

"It doesn't change the fact that I made a mistake once. I don't want to go down that road again."

His mom made a gruff sound in her throat and shook her head. "It's your life, and you can do what you want with it. I just don't wanna see you makin' a mistake. You're a different man than you were when you proposed right out of high school. You grew and changed, but she didn't. And that's okay. Not everybody's meant to stay together forever, but that doesn't mean you can't try again with someone else. I don't want you to throw away something that makes you happy just because you're stuck livin' in the past."

He didn't know why it took those words from his mom to snap him out of it and make him see reason, but it was as if she'd held a mirror in front of his face and made him open his eyes. He'd been looking at the past, focusing on what his life had been and all the mistakes he didn't want to repeat instead of looking to the future with Sadie. He didn't care how little time it'd taken for him to get to this point. He'd spent years before, when it all had amounted to nothing in the end.

In his bones, he knew Sadie was right for him. He only hoped he hadn't fucked up too much for her to give him another chance. He glanced down at his watch, cringing at the late hour and mentally calculating the drive back to Havenbrook.

"I gotta go," he said, bending to kiss his mom and sister on their cheeks.

"Nice work, Momma," Carly said, high-fiving their mom as Cole strode toward the front door. "I thought for sure it'd take a couple conversations before he pulled his head out of his ass."

His head was definitely out of his ass now. He just hoped he could make it to Sadie before the ball dropped at midnight.

CHAPTER 18

C ole didn't even want to think about how many traffic laws he broke speeding back to Havenbrook, but he didn't care if it cost him a thousand dollars in fines so long as he made it to Sadie in time. In an ideal situation, he would've had time to swing by his house. Put on a suit and plead his case to her in the way she deserved. Unfortunately, this wasn't an ideal situation, and he was racing against the clock, the time ticking too close to midnight for his comfort. So, he bypassed his home and sped straight to the historic center where they were holding this year's ball, hoping no one would still be taking tickets this late in the party.

He threw his car into park in the middle of a fire lane and raced up the front steps and into the building, not stopping until he crashed through the double doors of the event hall. The space was crowded, filled with Havenbrook residents in their finest. This year's theme was A Masked

Affair, so everyone inside wore one, cloaking half their faces.

Not that it mattered—almost immediately, Cole was able to spot Sadie from across the room. Even if it weren't for her vibrant red hair spilling down around her face, he'd still be able to find her. He hummed whenever they were in the vicinity of each other, his body aware of her every move. He'd ignored it for so long, pushed it out of his mind as if that were all it would take to forget about her. But now that he'd accepted it, his body came alive in her presence.

"This is the latest arrival I've ever seen," Edna said, perched on a chair by the door, a jar filled with tickets in front of her.

So much for that wish.

He ran a hand through his hair, taking his gaze off Sadie only long enough to attempt to sweet-talk Edna. "I don't have a ticket."

"I can see that, sugar. Don't have a suit either, apparently." She clucked her tongue and eyed him up and down, a slow shake to her head.

"Not a lot of time to swing by and grab it."

"No?" she asked. "Why's that?"

"I need to get to Sadie before midnight."

A slow smile swept across her face as she leaned toward him. "It was the carriage ride, wasn't it? I knew it. I've got a knack for pushin' two people together who're meant to be." She stood and pressed a hand to his back, not so subtly shoving him into the room. "Go on, now. And hurry. It's almost midnight."

"Thanks, Edna. I owe you one."

"You remember that the next time I get into another snafu," she called after him.

He shook his head, breathing out a laugh as his gaze sought out Sadie once again. She'd moved, somehow inching even farther from him, and urgency gripped his throat as he glanced at his watch. Six minutes.

"Mr. Donovan," a woman called as he passed.

He glanced over to find Aubrey Hayward, the woman from the shelter he'd spoken to a couple weeks prior. While he kept an eye on Sadie as she moved through the room, he said, "Please, I told you to call me Cole."

"Cole." She smiled warmly and lifted the two flutes of champagne she carried and gestured to a man who stood a few feet away. "I'm gonna ring in the new year with my husband, but I just wanted to thank you again for offerin' your services. We're so grateful."

"Of course. I'm happy to help however I can. I look forward to meetin' with you next week," he said before excusing himself and striding toward Sadie.

He couldn't tell if the lightness in his chest was because he felt a new sense of purpose in his career, or because he moved closer to Sadie with each step he took. Both, he decided, smiling for the first time since he'd last been with her.

Still halfway across the room from where she stood, he recognized the asshole from the inn sidling up to her. He clenched his jaw at the prick's audacity. She'd already told him no, several times. And, despite it being fake a couple weeks ago, had mentioned she had a boyfriend. Cole curled his hands into fists and forced his way through the crowd faster than before. Sadie stood, arms crossed, her negative body language rolling off her in waves, but the other guy didn't take a hint. He inched closer to her as midnight loomed, and Cole had absolutely no doubt this bastard was going to attempt to make a move when the clock struck twelve.

Cole strode up until her arm brushed his chest, and he exhaled a sigh of relief at the contact, not realizing until that moment just how much he'd needed it. Glaring daggers at the man invading Sadie's space, he said, "It should be enough for a woman to tell you no, but that's apparently not the case with you. Either you're too stupid or too arrogant to get it through your head when she says she's not interested, but let me make this perfectly clear for you. She's taken. Now, fuck off."

The guy shot wide eyes toward him, swallowing so hard Cole could practically hear it, even over the music and murmur of voices. He sputtered and nodded, his face reddening as he turned and faded into the crowd. Cole wouldn't be upset in the slightest if that was the last time he ever had to see that asshole.

Sadie twisted to face him, her mask hiding half her features, and gave him a quick once-over. "Thanks. You didn't need to do that, but I appreciate it. Hopefully that'll buy me at least a couple weeks."

Someone jostled him from behind, and he bumped into her, wrapping his arm around her waist and holding her against him. How could he have ever questioned if this was right? How could he have ever doubted they were supposed to be together? That his place was right here, next to her? Everything settled inside him as soon as she was in his arms, a peace he'd never known sweeping over him.

He leaned down until his lips were next to her ear, wanting to be certain she heard him over all the noise in the crowded room. "What if it bought you more than that?"

Pushing against his chest, she pulled back and looked up into his eyes. "What do you mean?"

He hated that he couldn't see her whole face, couldn't read her expressions. Couldn't tell from her tone alone what she was thinking. So he twined their fingers together and tugged her through the crowd until they reached a tiny alcove. He tucked them inside before reaching up and lifting her mask. Relieved to be able to see her face, though it didn't help. Her expression gave nothing away, which meant he didn't know if he was about to make the biggest fool of himself or not. But he also didn't care.

This chance with her was worth any possible failure he could face, and he wasn't going to leave here tonight until she knew exactly how he felt. Namely, that somehow, in the past few weeks—or hell, few years—he'd fallen in love with the woman who drove him crazy and settled his soul all at once.

"I fucked up, Sadie."

Surprise flickered in her eyes. "How?"

Shaking his head, he reached for her hand, dancing her fingers between his. "I was stupid, and I allowed my sham of a marriage to cast a shadow over what we have. I got scared because I spent years of my life with someone, only for that to end in a fiery crash. And I couldn't see how this could possibly be any different, especially when we've only really known each other for a short time."

She swallowed, her blue eyes gazing up at him, and he needed more contact with her than just holding her hand. He delved his fingers into her hair, cupping her face as he brushed his thumbs along her jaw. Needing this connection to her as he bared his heart.

"I can't promise you forever because I don't know what the future will hold for us. But I can promise you right now. And right now, I'd love nothing more than to kiss you at midnight, if you'll let me."

A sheen of tears coated her eyes, making them sparkle under the twinkling lights hanging from the ceiling. "Are you sure about that?" she asked, her eyes intent on his. Studying him. Reading his reactions.

"Surer than I've been about anything. I've been more miserable this past week without you than I ever have before. I've missed you, firecracker. I've missed your smart little mouth and your teasing jabs and that look you get in your eyes right before you—"

She reached up, pressing her hand against his mouth to stop his words as she darted her gaze around to the room packed full of Havenbrook residents. "Maybe you can stop bein' a pervert for five minutes and keep this PG?"

He smiled and pressed a kiss to the palm of her hand before she slid it down and rested it against his chest. "I can do that right now, but I can't make any guarantees about later."

"I see that confidence hasn't wavered at all."

"This isn't confidence. It's pure, undiluted hope."

She bit her lips, her fingers curling in the material of his T-shirt and spreading a wave of heat through his entire body. "You know a kiss at midnight means you're supposed to spend the next year with that person."

He pressed a hand to the small of her back and brought their bodies flush against each other, desperate to feel her in ways that were wholly inappropriate for the location they were currently in. The sound of the countdown rang out around them as he leaned down until his mouth hovered above hers, needing her to know how certain he was. Needing her to know that he wanted to go all in with her, and he didn't have a single doubt about it.

With every word he spoke, his lips brushed hers, and he hoped she felt exactly how deeply he meant each one. "A year won't be enough, but we can start with that."

EPILOGUE

It was amazing what a year could change. Sadie and Elise's entire world had been turned upside down when the edition of *Happily Ever After* featuring Sadie and Cole's images came out. Nat had kept up her end of the promise, the Starlight Haven Inn mentioned prominently in the piece, and their phone hadn't stopped ringing since. Not only were their rooms booked steadily, but they were also booked out a year for weddings. Having this kind of breathing room was exactly what Sadie had been hoping for when she'd agreed to do the spread in the first place.

With deposits secured out a year, that had allowed them to not only hire a full-time innkeeper, but it also made it so each of them could focus on what they loved. Sadie had transitioned to strictly wedding planning, and Elise... Well, Elise was still trying to figure out what she wanted to do, but at least she had the freedom now to do that. And best of all, their relationship had mended, the two of them growing closer in the time they'd spent apart. Turned out working together every day hadn't been good for them. Who knew?

It was almost six, and Cole was due to pick her up at the inn any minute so they could head out to the Sip and Shop event that evening. For the first year since they'd taken over ownership, neither she nor Elise needed to stay on the property tonight, and Sadie intended to take full advantage of that. She'd made up several batches of muffins this afternoon—she loved baking, and not even the switch from inn management to wedding planning could stop her from offering that once in a while—but that was the extent of it this year, and she was more relieved than she'd anticipated.

Cole had called her around lunchtime and let her know he had something that had come up and he'd be a little late to pick her up, but he'd be there as soon as he could. And she didn't doubt he would be. Since New Year's Eve last year, he'd never given her a reason to second-guess him. He'd been there, through the easy times as well as the rough patches, and she loved him more than she ever thought possible.

A rhythmic beeping sounded outside the inn, and Sadie furrowed her brow as she glanced out the front window. A large truck bearing Rory and Nash's company, King Haven Construction and Design, backed into the driveway, stopping as close to the front door as possible. And standing there, guiding the entire endeavor, was none other than Cole.

She grabbed her coat and slipped it on as she walked outside, her breath puffing in clouds in front of her. "Cole? What're you doin'? And why is Edna drivin' that truck?"

"Hey, sugar!" Edna called with a wave, poking her head out the window before she slammed on the brakes and jerked the entire truck to a halt.

Cole walked to the back and unlatched the door, glancing over at Sadie with a look in his eye she couldn't quite decipher. "Remember how I told you I had something come up this afternoon, so I'd be late?"

"Um...yeah?"

"Well, I was doin' a little reconnaissance."

Sadie's eyebrows lifted. "And Edna helped you with that?"

"Helped him? I'm the one who told him about it!" she called from where she still sat in the truck.

"Edna," Cole said with a sigh. "What'd we agree upon?"

The older woman huffed, and Sadie could practically hear her pout from there. "That I sit here and look pretty while you do all the work."

"That's right."

"I just wanna make sure I get some credit is all."

Cole chuckled under his breath and shook his head. "I'll make sure you do." Then, to Sadie, he said, "I owe her for this, but she's a real pain in my ass sometimes."

"I heard that!"

"I meant for you to."

Sadie rolled her eyes and stuffed her hands in her

pockets, already feeling the nip in the air. "If you two are done bickerin', maybe one of y'all can tell me what's goin' on."

"Like I was sayin', I did a little scopin' out earlier today. Seems Alec has a yearly poker game with some pretty hefty stakes."

"Alec...as in Elise's ex-husband? What the hell were you hangin' out with him for?"

"Did I ever tell you my mom taught me how to play poker? Said I needed to learn so I could win some spendin' money while I was away at college."

Sadie laughed and shook her head, though she wasn't surprised. Cole's momma was a spitfire who'd done what she had to to make ends meet. Sadie had come to love her in the year she and Cole had been together. "You didn't, but I'm not sure what that has to do with what you and Edna got up to this afternoon, or why Rory and Nash's truck is backed into the inn's driveway."

"I'm gettin' there."

"Get there faster—I'm freezin'."

"Yes, ma'am," he said, bending down to press a kiss to her lips. One that didn't last nearly long enough before he pulled away. "This probably won't surprise you, but Alec's a cocky little fuck, and he was all too willin' to put up exactly what I asked for in the last bet of the afternoon." Cole unlatched the doors and swung them open to reveal a packed backend full of...

Her family's antiques?

"Cole..." she breathed, stepping closer and running her

fingers over the smooth mahogany of her grandmother's old writing desk. The one she'd sat at with her as a child, practicing her ABC's. A lump formed in her throat, and tears pricked her eyes. Every single piece Alec had taken from her family was inside—the armoire that'd once held her grandma's clothes, the sewing machine passed down from her great-great-grandma, the grandfather clock she'd come to associate with staying with her grandparents. All of it was right there in front of her when she'd resigned herself to never seeing them again. "How did you do this?"

He stepped up behind her and wrapped an arm around her shoulders, tugging her back into his chest. Pressing a kiss to her temple, he held her close. "Like I said, he's an arrogant shit. I just had to put up something really good against all this, and he was all too willin' to pony up."

"What'd you bet?"

"My car."

Sadie's mouth dropped open, and she spun around to face him. "Wait, your *car*? The one you love more than me that you just bought three months ago?"

Cole rolled his eyes and reached a hand into his pocket. "First of all, I do not love it more than you. And second, yes."

"I wouldn't be so sure about that."

"What? That I love it more than you?"

"Yes. You even named it. How is *Claudette* doin' today, anyway?"

"She's fine, and so what? Lots of people name their cars. I don't sleep with it every night, do I?"

"Well, no. But—"

"And I don't make sweet, sweet love to it either, do I?"

She scoffed. "I'd hardly call what you do to me makin' sweet, sweet—"

"And I also didn't buy it one of these and plan to ask it to spend the rest of its life with me, did I?"

"You...what?" she asked, her brow furrowed. But then he grabbed her left hand and slipped something onto the third finger, and she froze. "Cole?"

He tugged her even closer, so there wasn't a breath of space between them, and lifted her hand to press a kiss against the ring he'd just slipped on. "Marry me."

She breathed out a laugh as tears stung her eyes, and her stomach did cartwheels. "You're supposed to ask me that, not demand it."

He shrugged, completely unrepentant, and kissed her. Long and deep, his tongue sweeping against her lower lip as he held her tight. Like even pressed up against her, they were too far apart. Like he never wanted to let her go.

Finally breaking away, he said, "I don't wanna ask because I don't wanna give you the idea I'd be okay with you sayin' no. I told you a long time ago I wasn't subtle or romantic. I want what I want, and I'm not afraid to go after it. And what I want is you." He cupped her face in his palms and pressed his lips to hers once more. "For the rest of my life. Say yes, firecracker."

She glanced down at the beautiful ring on her finger, then up at the man who'd completely and utterly stolen her heart, soul, and every ounce of her being. "You may

not be subtle, but I hate to tell you...this is romantic as
hell."

"I told you!" Edna yelled from the truck. "Now, are
you gonna answer him already?"

Cole squeezed his eyes shut as Sadie giggled, her heart
in her throat as a tear trailed down her cheek. "Well? Are
you gonna put us both out of our misery, or should I grab a
chair and camp out here for the night?"

She bit her lip and darted her eyes between his,
looking for any apprehension on his part. Any hesitation or
uncertainty. But she didn't find it anywhere. All she saw
when she looked into his eyes was the same thing she knew
he saw in hers. Pure, unconditional love.

"I don't know," she said, wrapping her arms around his
neck and admiring the sparkle of the stone under the twinkling lights outside. "What if you drive me crazy for the
rest of my life?"

"Oh, I'd count on it, firecracker."

"Give the poor man a yes!" Edna yelled.

Sadie laughed against Cole's lips as he stared down at
her, eyes sparkling. "After bribing me with all these
antiques, how could I say no?"

"I wasn't above doin' that if it meant I got to call you
mine forever. Does that mean your answer's a yes?"

"You know it is. With you, it's always yes."

Edna whooped in the cab of the truck as a grin split
Cole's face. He kissed her, slipping his tongue into her
mouth when she parted her lips on a sigh. Sadie had spent
her life dreaming about this very thing—a forever kind of

love she wouldn't give up for anything. The kind that made her toes curl and her heart sing. That drove her crazy and soothed her all at once.

Cole was her forever, her happily ever after. And she was his.

ABOUT THE AUTHOR

USA Today and *Wall Street Journal* bestselling author Brighton Walsh spent a decade as a professional photographer before taking her storytelling in a different direction and reconnecting with her first love—writing. She likes her books how she likes her tea—steamy and satisfying—and adores strong-willed heroines and the protective heroes who fall head over heels for them. Brighton lives in the Midwest with her real life hero of a husband, her two kids—both taller than her—and her dog who thinks she's a queen. Her boy-filled house is the setting for dirty socks galore, frequent dance parties (okay, so it's mostly her, by herself, while her children look on in horror), and more laughter than she thought possible.

www.brightonwalsh.com
brighton@brightonwalsh.com

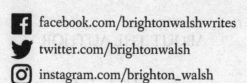

facebook.com/brightonwalshwrites

twitter.com/brightonwalsh

instagram.com/brighton_walsh